# Katie's

## Amish Journey of Hope

THE AMISH WOMEN OF
LAWRENCE COUNTY SERIES - BOOK 8

Tracy Fredrychowski

ISBN: 979-8-9919988-4-0 (paperback)
ISBN: 979-8-9919988-3-3 (digital)

Cover Design by Tracy Lynn Virtual, LLC



Published in South Carolina by The Tracer Group, LLC
https://tracyfredrychowski.com

Katie's Amish Journey of Hope

# PROLOGUE

*September - Willow Springs, Pennsylvania*

The noise on the other side of the door only made my anxiety worse as I pressed my back against it. Ella's little fists tapped rapidly, followed by her sweet voice. "*Mamm*, are you coming out? We're hungry."

Mary's voice chimed in, more impatient. "You said we could have snack time after we finished coloring."

And then came Ella, her tiny toddler feet thudding against the door as she let out a loud wail. "*Mamm*!"

I clenched my eyes shut, clutching the letter in my hand. The familiar texture of the worn paper was both a comfort and a reminder of how many times I'd read these words, hoping for strength. But the strain of *Mamm's* absence was heavier than the comfort her words could bring.

*Put Gott first. Be a loving mother. Honor your husband. Be his helpmate.*

Each line felt like a task I wasn't strong enough to complete. How could I put *Gott* first when I felt so lost? How could I be a loving mother when I could barely get through the day? And as for honoring my husband, it felt like I was failing Daniel more with each passing moment.

Ella's wails grew louder, her tiny fists joining her *schwesters'* knocks. "*Maaaamm*!"

"Shhh," Mary whispered. "*Mamm's* coming soon."

"Maybe she's crying again," Mary added in a quieter voice.

The guilt twisted in my stomach, sharp and unforgiving. My precious children. They didn't understand why their mother wasn't the same anymore, why I spent so much time locked away in this bathroom, clinging to a tattered letter like it held all the answers.

"I'll be out in a minute," I called, though my voice cracked.

I unfolded the letter, my eyes scanning *Mamm's* familiar handwriting. Even now, her words felt like a lifeline, even if they couldn't pull me out of this dark place.

*You were chosen for this life, Katie, to love, to nurture, to build a home filled with joy and faith.*

But what if I couldn't do it? What if the pieces of me that *Mamm* believed in were gone, buried under layers of sorrow and pain?

Ella's sobs softened into hiccups, but the sound of the *kinner* waiting on the other side of the door was enough to force me to my feet. In the distance, I heard Danny stirring from his morning nap, crying out to be nursed. I carefully folded the letter and slipped it into my pocket, close to my heart but hidden from view.

*Mamm's* words echoed in my ears, adding a fresh round of sobs in the back of my throat as I played them over in my head.

*I know someday I won't be here to walk with you through life's joys and sorrows. That thought is difficult for me, as I imagine it will be for you. When that time comes, I want you to remember that it's natural to grieve, my sweet girl. Sorrow is a reflection of how deeply you love, but it is not meant to consume you. When the pain feels heavy, lean into Gott's strength, just as I have in my hardest moments. He will carry you, even when you feel like you cannot take another step.*

I placed my hand on the doorknob and took a deep breath. "Alright, I'm coming. Let's get you both that snack before I tend to the *boppli*."

My voice sounded steadier than I felt, but maybe that was enough. For now, it had to be.

# CHAPTER 1

The baby's cry broke through the pre-dawn stillness, thin and urgent. Daniel stirred with a groan, one hand reaching across the bed for his *fraa*. His fingers met only the cool rumple of empty sheets.

"Katie?" he murmured into the stillness.

No answer.

He pushed up on one elbow, blinking at the wind-up clock on the dresser. Just past five. Danny's usual feeding time. The child's cry sharpened into a wail, pulling Daniel fully upright.

He bent over and lifted the squirming bundle from the bassinet. The boy's tiny face was red and scrunched, his fists flailing under the blanket. Daniel held the child away from his chest, preventing the child's soiled clothes from penetrating his own.

With practiced hands, he carried the baby to the changing table and worked quickly, murmuring softly. "It's alright, *sohn*.

We'll get you dry, *jah*?"

Fresh diaper, clean blanket, arms wrapped snug. The boy's cries softened but didn't stop. "Let's go find your *mamm*."

Daniel cradled him close and moved through the dim hallway and down the stairs, checking the kitchen, the front room, and the bathroom. Empty. The knot in his chest tightened.

It had only been two weeks since his mother-in-law Ruth passed, and the shadow of it still hung in the air like smoke after a fire. Katie hadn't been the same. Not that he blamed her. But she was slipping farther from him each day, and he was trying… truly trying to be patient. To love her through something he couldn't fix.

He opened the front door and stepped onto the porch. There she was, curled on the swing, knees drawn to her chest beneath her nightdress. A blue shawl hung loosely over her shoulders, slipping down one arm. Her bare feet were tucked close, her whole body folded in as if trying to disappear. The swing barely moved. Her face was turned toward the pasture, streaked with silent tears.

The cool air met him with a damp whisper, speaking softly of fall's slow approach. The wind carried the earthy scent of fading summer, cut hay, damp soil, the faint perfume of goldenrod and drying mint. Mist clung to the fencerows like a veil, and the horizon glowed with the faintest light, September's promise of change.

Daniel crossed the porch and adjusted the *boppli* in his arms. "There you are. He's hungry."

Katie turned toward him, her eyes glassy and rimmed with red. She reached for the child without speaking. As soon as Danny was at her breast, his cries melted into soft, contented sounds.

The swing creaked beneath them, slow and mournful. A rooster called somewhere near the barn, sharp against the hush of morning.

"You should've woken me, you didn't have to be out here alone."

"I couldn't sleep." Katie's voice barely rose above the baby's gentle suckling. "I keep thinking I hear her calling my name. Like she's still here. Then I go look and… nothing."

Daniel's throat tightened. "I'm sorry."

He stared out at the pasture. The trees stood quiet and watchful in the fog. He wished he had words… real ones that could soothe her. But everything inside him felt clumsy and small beside the ache she carried.

"I've got to head out soon," he murmured, eyes drifting toward the barn. "Those two new racers are coming early. Need time to settle them before I start their buggy work."

Katie nodded, her eyes still fixed on the gray light creeping into the sky.

"I'll come in for breakfast after chores."

"I don't think I'll make breakfast," she murmured.

Daniel hesitated, then rested his hand on her shoulder. "I'll figure something out."

He stood slowly, reluctant to leave her there on the swing, but the morning was calling, and the baby was fed for now. He shifted his weight, hesitating.

"I need to get dressed. I'll put the coffee on… and I'll wake Mary to help with Ella's breakfast."

Katie didn't answer, but her grip on the baby shifted just slightly, tighter, maybe. Resigned. He knew it wasn't much, but it was the only thing he could think to offer her right now.

Daniel walked back inside, the screen door creaking shut behind him. The house was still dim, shadows lingering in the corners as the gray light of morning began to push its way in. He moved through the kitchen in silence, filling the kettle and setting it on the stove. The aroma of coffee grounds, rich and bitter, was one of the few familiar comforts he could still count on.

As the water heated, he made his way down the hallway toward the girls' room. He paused at the door, resting one hand on the frame. For a moment, he listened to the supple breaths on the other side, the rustle of sleep.

He hated waking her. Mary was just five. She should be outside chasing butterflies, or gathering wildflowers along the creek bank, not pulling stools over to the counter or helping her little *schwester* get dressed.

But the truth was, Mary had stepped up in a way no one had asked her to. And now he was about to ask even more.

The knot in his chest twisted tighter. Guilt pinched at him as he gently pushed open the door.

"Mary," he whispered, keeping his voice low as he knelt beside her bed. "Can you help with Ella this morning? *Mamm's* really tired, and I've got to head out soon."

She blinked up at him, pulling her favorite fuzzy blanket to her chin, and nodded without a word.

He patted her forehead and tried to smile. "*Dankie*. You're such a big help."

As he stood to head out to the barn, he cast one glance back toward the porch. Katie was still there, a shadowed figure wrapped in a blue shawl, cradling their son against the cool hush of a morning that had already asked too much of all of them.

***

The creak of the porch swing had slowed to stillness. Katie didn't know how long she'd been sitting there. The shawl was damp along her back, clinging to her nightdress from the veil of early morning dew, but she hadn't noticed the chill.

The *boppli* had fallen asleep in her arms, his lips still pursed in the rhythm of nursing. His tiny breath warmed the fabric at her chest, his hand curled against her like a small anchor tethering her to a world she didn't want to rejoin.

Her eyes had blurred as she stared into the mist-softened trees across the pasture. In her mind, she could almost hear the low hum of her *mamm's* voice beside her, fingers flying over the stretched quilt frame, the gentle click of needles, and the fragrance of lavender oil always on her skin.

Every Friday morning, the two of them would sit in her mother's sewing room and work on the quilt for a few hours.

Now the latest sat unfinished, still stretched in the frame, abandoned in a corner of her mother's favorite place.

She might've sat there until noon if not for the crash.

The sound startled her so badly that she gasped, jerking upright. The sharp crack of breaking pottery echoed from the kitchen.

Katie stood quickly, heart racing. Danny stirred but didn't wake. She slipped inside and laid him lightly on the small daybed tucked in the corner of the kitchen, bracing his side with a folded quilt. The warmth of his weight still lingered on her chest.

Mary stood frozen, her small hands clasped in front of her as she stared at the shattered pieces of a cereal bowl scattered across the floor. Ella sat wide-eyed at the table, her legs swinging above the floor.

Without a word, Katie grabbed a broom and dustpan from behind the woodstove. The girls watched her in silence as she swept up the shards.

Mary's voice was barely a whisper. "I didn't mean to."

Katie knelt beside the last few pieces. "I know, it's alright."

But their eyes didn't lift. They only watched her… quiet, cautious, as if they feared she might shatter too.

A knock broke the stillness.

Katie stood and emptied the dustpan into the trash. Through the wavy glass of the door, she saw the familiar stoop of her father's shoulders, the worn brim of his straw hat cupped in his hands. His presence there, so early, made her chest tighten.

She opened the door.

Her father looked like a man both lost and determined. His beard looked like it hadn't seen a comb since the funeral.

He nodded once in greeting. "Mornin', Katie."

She moved aside so he could come in. He didn't make it past the threshold.

"I—I need your help." He lowered his eyes and twirled his hat in his hands. "I thought maybe you could clean out your mother's things in the bedroom."

Katie's heart dropped into her stomach.

Levi cleared his throat, his voice rougher than usual. "I left some boxes for you in the hallway. I'll haul them down to the secondhand store in Willow Springs on Monday."

She didn't trust her voice.

Her fingers curled into the fabric of her nightdress as she nodded. "I'll come over later this morning."

He looked like he might say more. But instead, he placed

his hat back on his head with trembling hands and turned back toward home. The door softly clicked closed behind him.

Katie moved to the window and watched as her father crossed the yard between their houses, his gait slower than usual, shoulders sagging beneath the pain he carried. He disappeared into the side door of the now-empty home where her mother's presence still lingered in every curtain and cupboard.

Samuel and Emma's house sat just across the lane, calm in the morning light. Beyond it, the fields her father tended stretched wide with rows of late strawberries browning under the dew, and the fall mums already bursting into rich blooms of rust, gold, and deep crimson.

The land was moving forward, dressed in the colors of a new season, as if the world hadn't noticed that all their hearts had stopped, silently and indefinitely, two weeks earlier.

***

The morning sun filtered through the window of Samuel and Emma's kitchen, shining light across the pine table where two coffee mugs sat cooling beside a worn Bible and a folded feed order. The quiet was only briefly interrupted by the three-year-old twins, Owen and Otto's playful racket. They had turned a flour sack into a cape and were now galloping around the *haus* like miniature horses. Cindy, just two and still half asleep, toddled into Emma's lap, thumb tucked in her mouth.

Samuel sat at the table, elbow resting on the page, but he wasn't reading.

"Didn't sleep again?" Emma asked softly as she brushed crumbs from the table into her palm.

He shrugged. "I sleep. Just not right."

Emma knew what he meant. A couple of weeks wasn't much time when you'd buried the woman who raised you. Not much time at all.

She looked at her husband's face, so like Levi's now in the way grief had settled into the lines. Samuel wasn't loud with his sorrow. He didn't wear it on his sleeve. He worked it out through his hands and feet, like his *datt* always had. And this morning would be no different.

"We've got a long day," he said as he reached for his mug. "Daniel said those new geldings will be skittish, barely out of racing shoes. We'll have our hands full getting them to take the harness."

"You like the challenge." Emma smiled gently.

"I like it when things make sense," he muttered.

Stillness settled again.

Emma looked down at Cindy, her hand absently brushing across her belly. She hadn't told Samuel yet. She didn't want to… not now. Not when everything felt fragile and thin. She'd wait. Let him grieve his *mamm* first.

"You going to check on Katie?" he asked as he stood and reached for his hat.

Emma nodded. "I thought I might offer to take the children for a while. Maybe give her a chance to breathe."

Samuel paused in the doorway. "If anyone can reach her, it's you."

She wished she could believe that. But Katie had been locked behind invisible walls since the funeral. Emma knew that pain. She remembered the numbness that followed her own *mamm's* passing. And she remembered the ache, that deep, hollowness that came when they'd lost their first baby five years ago.

Trusting in *Gott's* plan hadn't erased the pain. It never did. But it helped her survive it.

After Samuel left for the barn, Emma dressed the children

and tucked a fresh loaf of bread into a basket with some apple butter and leftover cheese curds. She fastened Cindy's bonnet and jacket, ignoring the tiny voice in her heart whispering, *Now might not be the right time to say anything to Katie.* She pressed a hand once more to her belly, silent and unsure.

They crossed the lane as the sunlight brightened over Levi's field. It looked like life was marching forward. But Emma knew better. Sometimes beauty bloomed even while hearts broke wide open.

After Emma softly knocked on the door, Katie opened it with the same blank look she'd worn at the funeral. Her *kapp* was askew, her hair loose at the nape, and Danny squirmed in one arm.

"I brought the *kinner* over," Emma said with cheer. "Thought maybe you'd like a little break."

Katie didn't smile. "I don't need a break," she exclaimed as she put Danny in his bouncy chair.

The sharpness in Katie's voice made Emma flinch beside her as she glanced over the messy kitchen. "I thought I'd stay a bit. Maybe let the *kinner* play some."

Emma crouched to take the basket from Otto and gently guided the children inside.

Katie hovered near the table, shifting the baby in her arms. Her voice was tight, almost brittle. "*Datt* came by. Asked me to go through *Mamm's* things. Maybe you could watch the *kinner* while I do that."

Emma looked up. "Do you want help?"

"*Nee*." Katie didn't meet her eyes.

Emma nodded slowly. "I'll stay with the *kinner*, no problem."

No, thank you, just a tight nod from Katie as she passed through the doorway and headed toward her parents' *haus*. Emma watched her go, the shawl slipping from one shoulder, her posture stiff as fence posts.

After Katie left, the house was too quiet for a place with five children. Owen and Otto had taken to stacking books on the floor. Cindy sat with a cloth doll clutched in her hands, and Ella stared at her toast but hadn't taken a bite as Mary tried to coax her into eating.

Emma moved among them gradually, silently filling the space Katie had left behind, letting her sister-in-law grieve the only way she knew how. With distance. With silence. With walls too high to climb.

***

Katie strode off her porch and crossed the yard just as her father was coming around the corner of his *haus*, a wrench in one hand and grease smudged on the hem of his shirt.

He gave a small nod.

She nodded back.

"I'll be out in the equipment shed. The planter's been sticking again. Holler if you need anything."

His voice was gruffer than usual. More like gravel than timber.

As he passed her, he hesitated. "I appreciate you doing this, I'm sorry I… I just can't do it myself."

He didn't wait for her to respond, just kept walking, his boots crunching toward the shed.

Katie stood still. The porch boards of her childhood home groaned as she stepped onto them. Her eyes drifted to the rocker where her *mamm* used to sit with a mending basket balanced on her lap, humming low and tuneless under her breath. The wind carried a hint of chrysanthemums from the side garden.

When she opened the door, the smell of lemon soap, dried herbs, and her mother's lavender sachet hit her like a wave.

It hadn't changed. The air inside was still, too still, as

though the house was holding its breath with her.

Her legs carried her down the hall on memory alone.

She paused in the doorway of the sewing room. Morning light streamed through the big window, warming the large quilt still stretched in the frame. The pattern, a bold blue-and-yellow dahlia, looked alive in the sunlight. The last thing her mother touched. The stitches were so delicate, Katie could barely tell where one ended and another began.

She reached out and laid her hand gently on the fabric, fingers brushing the soft cotton as if it might still hold warmth. A sob caught in her throat, and she bit it back.

Her mother's thimble sat on the edge of the windowsill, catching the light like a sliver of memory.

Katie turned, opened the cupboard, and found an old flat sheet. She draped it carefully over the quilt, shielding it from the sunlight's fading touch. It didn't feel right to put it away.

The hallway to the bedroom felt longer than it used to. Or maybe she was just moving slower.

The door creaked open. The room was neat. Still lived-in. Her mother's prayer covering and nightdress still hung on a wooden peg near the bed. Her scent, lavender and clean linen, still lingered in the folds.

Katie's hands shook as she reached for the first drawer.

She wasn't sure she could do this. But she also knew no one else could. She bowed her head.

"I don't understand this, Lord," she sighed. "But I'm here." And in that small surrender, between the ache and the restraint, she began packing away her mother's things.

# CHAPTER 2

The next day, Katie climbed into the seat, wrapping her shawl tighter as she waited for Daniel to hand up the baby. Danny was already fussing, squirming against the bundle of blankets, but she took him and cradled him close with practiced arms. Daniel brushed her hand briefly before leading the horse and buggy away from the barn.

The last place she wanted to be was in a crowded farmhouse for a three-hour church service. But she was going. That's what was expected. And sometimes doing what was expected was easier than explaining why she couldn't.

Tension ran high all morning as they tiptoed around each other, preparing the *kinner* for church. Her harsh words still lingered in the air between them, leaving a heaviness in the closed-in buggy.

The wheels crunched softly over the gravel drive as Daniel pulled the horse to a stop in front of the Zook farm. The yard was already full of buggies tucked in tight rows along the fencerow, brown canvas tops catching the early light like rows of resting beetles. The gentle clip and shuffle of hooves drifted from the corral where the horses stood tethered, tails flicking.

Inside the Zook home, the benches had been set up in rows that spilled from the kitchen into the living room. Women to one side, men to the other. The smell of freshly scrubbed pine floors mingled with the familiar aromas of a Sunday meal in waiting… bean soup simmering in iron kettles on the back stove, fresh loaves of bread stacked in towel-covered baskets, pickled beets, and cinnamon apple schnitz lined up in serving dishes near the sink.

The room was balmy. Too warm as Katie shifted the baby as she settled on the bench between Emma and another neighbor woman. Her heavy cape dress itched. Her stomach churned. The smell of the soup, heavy and rich, turned her nausea into a rolling wave.

The minister's voice droned on, slow and rhythmic, as he read from Corinthians. Katie tried to focus. Tried to still her hands and still her thoughts. She couldn't.

The baby stirred, restless, and she rose slowly and began to edge down the side aisle between the benches. As she passed

Daniel, sitting two rows over with Samuel, their eyes met.

*Are you alright?* he mouthed.

Katie shifted the baby and mouthed back, *I need air.*

He gave a small nod as she turned toward the back door. Outside, the cool breeze hit her face like a balm. She walked onto the porch and sank down on the top step, letting Danny rest against her shoulder. His breathing steadied. The fresh air quieted her stomach.

From the corral came the gentle sound of horses shifting, nickering softly. The wind rustled through the dried cornstalks in the far field, and through the open windows behind her, the slow, deep harmony of the congregation's hymn floated like a sigh. She closed her eyes.

"*Ach*, Katie." The voice was low and heartfelt, wrapped in years and understanding. "You slipped out, did you?"

Katie opened her eyes to see Betty Troyer, an older widow from their district, coming up the path. She was smoothing her apron and tucking a small handkerchief into her sleeve, having just come from the outhouse.

"Not everyone takes kindly to the smell of soup before the preacher's done talking," Betty said with a knowing smile as she eased herself onto the step beside Katie.

Katie let out the smallest breath that might have once been a laugh.

Betty tilted her head slightly, studying her. "These first weeks are like walking on barn ice. Nothing feels sturdy underfoot. But you're upright, and that's something."

Katie didn't answer.

Betty patted her arm lightly. "The Lord don't mind if you step outside once in a while, so long as you're still listening."

Katie nodded, her eyes fixed on the buggies lined in tidy rows. The world around her was orderly; however, she felt anything but.

***

Katie sat on a low stool in the far corner of the Zook kitchen, tucked beside the dry sink where a faded quilt had been hung for privacy. Danny nursed softly, his small hand fisted against the bodice of her dress. The clamor of footsteps and voices surrounded her, heavy shoes on wooden floors, plates clinking, children laughing, and benches scooting across the floor being arranged for the noontime meal.

The men had begun filling the long tables, hats left on the

front porch, heads bowed as one of the ministers led a short, silent grace. In the kitchen, the women moved like clockwork, skirts swishing, aprons fluttering, voices low but constant as they passed bowls of warm soup and thick slices of bread to be served.

"Katie," came a voice to her left, soft but purposeful. It was Mariam Kauffman, a woman near her *mamm's* age with a gentle face and the kind of eyes that always looked like they knew more than they should. "It's *goot* to see you here today. I know it's not easy, but you're showing strength in just coming."

Katie managed a tight nod, shifting Danny in her arms.

Another voice chimed in, Leona Shetler, never one to soften her opinions. "When my *mamm* passed, I thought I'd never stop crying. But tears don't feed the chickens, and misery doesn't bring the dead back. Time and the Lord are both good healers if we let 'em be."

"It's alright to mourn," Mariam added kindly. "But we mustn't stay in sorrow too long. It can lead to doubting His will."

Leona added, "The Lord gives, and the Lord takes away. Trusting that is part of our witness."

Katie kept her focus on her *sohn*, pretending she didn't hear the subtle edge in their words.

They meant well. She knew that. She truly did. But every word landed like a stone pressing beneath her ribs.

*How long was too long to grieve?* She wondered.

Would they still say these things if they'd heard her crying into her mother's quilt in the dark? Or watched her little girl gently wipe her tears on the sleeve of her own dress?

Mariam moved to Katie's side. "Eat. You're feeding a *boppli*, and that takes strength in itself."

Katie opened her mouth to reply, but nothing came. She suddenly couldn't breathe in that corner. Couldn't hear over the ache pounding in her chest.

And then… Emma's voice.

"There you are." Emma stepped into the kitchen with a knowing smile. "I thought you might like some fresh air again."

Katie looked up. Emma's eyes didn't ask questions. They just offered an escape.

With a nod, Katie rose and adjusted the baby on her shoulder. The other women parted to let her pass, still murmuring well-wishes behind her.

Emma gently caught her arm. "There's shade under that big maple tree by the corral. The children are already out there. I'll bring you a plate."

Katie didn't answer, but her body moved in that direction. Away from the words. Away from their well-meaning advice.

***

Daniel stepped into the Zook house just behind Samuel, the low hum of voices already thick. The men were filing in now, lining the benches as steaming bowls of bean soup made their way down the table.

"Looks like we've got another round of horses coming Tuesday," Samuel tilted his head toward Daniel. "That bay gelding from Middlefield, too."

Daniel nodded absently, his eyes drifting toward the back of the kitchen.

The side door creaked open just slightly, just enough for him to see Katie slipping out, her shawl clutched tight around her shoulders, the baby curled against her chest. He paused.

The impact of their argument that morning still sat heavy across his ribs like a board he hadn't been able to shift. The ride over had been mostly silent, sharp words spoken too early, apologies swallowed before they could reach the air.

It felt like no matter what he did, whether he gave her space or stayed close, he was wrong.

Samuel didn't notice his distraction as he recalled his own family's morning commotion. "Otto dumped a whole cup of milk down Cindy's back this morning. Emma didn't even blink. Just changed her and sent them out the door."

Daniel forced a slight smile. "That's my *schwester* for you… a strong one for sure and certain."

Samuel clapped him on the back. "Same as you."

Daniel didn't reply.

The tension between him and Katie wasn't angry. It was something deeper, something more tangled. Her grief had become a wall, and though he pressed his weight against it every day, it never gave. She didn't let him in… not really.

He hadn't told Samuel about the nights he lay awake listening to her crying into her pillow. Or how sometimes she wouldn't speak to him until noon. Or how the sharpness in her tone was never about the bread left out or the bucket left unwashed… it was about something far heavier. Something he couldn't reach.

The hardest part was knowing she wasn't herself. She was simply hurting, and he had no place to set that pain down for her.

Samuel pointed toward the empty spots near the window. "You want to sit, or wait for the second table?"

Daniel watched the side yard through the open door for just a second longer. Katie was already halfway to the maple tree, her shoulders hunched, the baby sleeping against her collarbone.

He wanted to go to her. Wanted to sit beside her in the grass and say nothing. Just be near her to ease her pain. But something told him to let her go. To let her have that time.

"I'll wait."

Samuel raised a brow. "Suit yourself."

Daniel sat on the bench near the back of the room, the scent of warm bread thick in the air, and folded his hands together, staring at his thumbs as they moved in slow circles.

*Help me reach her, Lord,* he prayed silently.

***

The rooster had already crowed twice, and her family was awake, but Katie wasn't.

Daniel stood in the center of the kitchen, holding a crying

baby in one arm and a lukewarm mug of coffee in the other. The girls sat at the table in yesterday's wrinkled dresses, hair half-pinned, waiting with tired eyes and empty bowls.

He looked up the stairs again. No sound from above.

"Should I go get *Mamm*?" Mary asked, her voice small.

"*Nee*, I'll try again."

He shifted the baby, handed him gently to Mary, who took her little *bruder* like she'd done it a hundred times already, and climbed the steps.

The door to their room was cracked open. The room was dim despite the morning sun pressing through the window. She was still curled on her side, her back to the door, motionless.

Daniel strode inside carefully. "Katie… I've got to get to the barn, Samuel is waiting for me, and the *kinner* need you."

"I can't." Her voice was muffled by the pillow.

He moved closer. "Just a few minutes. They need you."

She rolled onto her back, eyes red and heavy. "Then you do it." Her voice cracked. "I don't have the strength today."

Daniel stood there for a moment. The edge in her voice stung more than he wanted to admit, but he knew better than to take it personally.

He turned to leave just as a soft knock came from the back

door downstairs.

By the time he reached the kitchen again, Betty Troyer was standing just inside the doorway, a casserole wrapped in a tea towel in her arms and a determined glint in her eyes.

She greeted them as she set the dish down on the counter. "It's baked oatmeal. Still warm with blueberries."

He looked at her… aproned, calm, no nonsense, and something in him relaxed. "*Dankie*. You didn't have to…"

"I did." She glanced toward the stairs. "Is she up?"

Daniel hesitated. "*Nee*."

"Did she eat yesterday?"

"I think she picked at supper."

"And the day before?"

Daniel rubbed the back of his neck. "I don't know."

Betty's look softened. "By the look on her face the other day, I knew she needed a visit, whether she realizes it or not."

Betty removed her sweater and hung it on the hook by the back door. "*Ach*, she's drowning in her own sorrow. That's normal. But we don't leave our people in deep waters… not in this community."

He nodded, not trusting his voice.

She turned, already reaching for bowls. "Go on. Get

yourself out to the barn. I'll see to the girls and then…" She glanced toward the ceiling, resolute. "Then I'll see to her."

Mary brightened at the sight of the hot dish, and Ella climbed onto the bench with a smile. Daniel paused in the doorway, watching Betty spoon oatmeal into bowls like it was the most natural thing in the world.

"*Dankie* again," he said as he handed Danny to her waiting arms.

She didn't look up. "Go on. I've got this part."

And he went, his steps heavy with worry, leaving behind the smell of warm blueberries and a woman who didn't believe in letting heartache win without a fight.

***

The door creaked when Daniel left, and he didn't bother to close it behind him. Katie stayed where she was, staring at the ceiling through swollen eyes, her body a weight she couldn't will into movement. Her ears strained past the stillness of her room to the voices drifting up from below. She struggled to place the voice, but finally she did, Betty.

The clink of dishes. The gentle rise and fall of her voice as she spoke to the girls in her usual cheerful way, steady, kind, capable. As if everything was fine and she hadn't stayed in bed while her daughters waited in the kitchen with tangled hair and rumbling bellies.

Mary laughed. Ella squealed. A knife went straight through Katie's heart. The guilt rose fast and fierce in her lungs until she could hardly breathe. What kind of mother couldn't even get out of bed to feed her *kinner*? What kind of *fraa* pushed away her own husband and her best friend? *One who has nothing left to give,* she told herself. *Not even to the ones who need her most.*

She pulled the quilt over her head like a shield, curling deeper into herself, trying to shut out the sounds of morning. But the heat of the blankets had gone cold. Her pillow no longer brought comfort. And the guilt, raw and constant, refused to be ignored. Thirty minutes passed. Maybe more.

And then, finally, with the effort of someone moving through deep water, she sat up. Her bones felt too heavy, her head too full. But she stood. She dressed. She pinned on a head covering with trembling fingers and made her way down the stairs.

The kitchen was cozy and smelled faintly of blueberries and cinnamon. Betty stood at the sink, humming under her breath as she rinsed a pot and handed Mary a dish towel. Ella sat with her chin resting in one hand, drawing circles in a puddle of spilled milk. Danny was cozy, bundled around Betty's ample waist with a baby sling, his tiny body swaying against her hip.

They all looked so… normal, like her absence hadn't left a gaping hole in the morning.

Betty turned when she heard Katie's steps on the floorboards. She didn't flinch at the sight of her. Didn't fuss or fawn. She just smiled like nothing was broken at all.

"We were just about to bring this little one up to you."

Katie opened her mouth, but nothing came. Betty moved forward and gently placed the baby into her arms.

"There now. He's hungry."

Katie pressed her cheek to his downy head, trying not to cry.

"Sit," Betty nodded toward a chair. "I've got something that'll help get you going this morning."

Katie hesitated but sat.

Betty poured hot water from the kettle and placed a mug in front of her, the scent of peppermint rising with the steam. Then she slid a plate across the table… one slice of toast, barely buttered at the edges.

"Not much, but it's a start," Betty murmured.

Katie wrapped one hand around the mug and nodded, too ashamed to meet her eyes.

Betty turned back to the sink, humming low.

She didn't press. She didn't scold. She simply stayed.

***

The morning had stretched long already, and the children had begun to turn restless.

Betty wiped her hands on her apron and turned to the girls. "Mary, why don't you take your *schwester* outside and gather the eggs? Take the small basket near the back door. The hens might give you a bit of fuss, but be brave."

Mary smiled, taking Ella's hand. The two slipped out into the crisp morning, the screen door clapping against the hinges behind them.

At the sink, Katie rinsed her mug. The water ran warm over her fingers, but her arms felt heavy. Her mind heavier still. She didn't realize how long she'd been staring until Betty's footsteps passed behind her and faded down the hallway.

A voice floated back. "Found the laundry pile."

Katie's stomach clenched. "*Nee*... you don't need to..."

But Betty reappeared, arms full of rumpled towels and dirty clothes. “Bathroom basket’s near tipping. And the girls don’t have any clean dresses. Best get it started.”

Katie’s cheeks burned. “I was going to get to it.”

“I know.” Betty’s voice was calm. “But today, we can do it together.”

Katie bit back the protest on her tongue, shame rising hot in her throat. Without speaking, she reached for the second basket, the bedsheets. The ones that hadn’t been washed for close to a month.

Together they moved down the stairs, footsteps creaking against worn wood. The air below was cool, edged with damp stone and the clean scent of lye soap. Katie dropped her basket beside the wringer washer, her hands stiff.

“I can’t even do my own laundry.”

“You can,” Betty replied, rolling up her sleeves. “Just not today.”

“It shouldn’t be this hard.”

Betty’s movements were collected. “*Nee*. But sometimes it is.”

A towel slipped from the pile and landed on the cold floor. Katie stared at it a moment before stooping to pick it up.

"I hate this. I hate that you have to... that I need help for things I used to do without thinking."

The generator hummed to life as Betty started the washer. "This isn't rescue. It's love."

Katie turned away, blinking hard. But Betty's voice followed her, even and sure.

"I've been where you are. When Abram passed I didn't rise from my bed for three days. My *dochder* sat beside me and I never spoke a word."

Katie swallowed. "I don't want your stories," she snapped. "I want my *mamm*."

The room held a long, thick reserve. Just the churn of water and the hum of the machine.

"I know. And if I could bring her back, I would. But since I can't—I'll help you stand again. However long it takes."

Katie pressed her hand to her forehead. The burn of tears gathered again, but something loosened inside her, just slightly. For the first time, her voice came quieter.

"I should be doing this myself."

Betty smiled kindly. "And soon you will."

Katie didn't thank her. Couldn't. Not yet. But when Betty reached for the next armful of sheets, Katie didn't turn away this time. She bent and gathered the next bundle with her own hands.

# CHAPTER 3

The squeal of rusted metal echoed through the equipment barn as Levi wrestled with the planter hitch again. The bolts refused to line up, and the lever, usually smooth as churned butter, jerked and caught under his grip.

Daniel stood nearby, one boot braced against the axle of the hay wagon, hands covered in grease and grit. He held back from stepping in for now.

Samuel, crouched on the other side of the frame, gave a slight glance up toward Daniel, his brow arched in question. It wasn't the first time his *datt* had fumbled a job recently that used to be second nature. It wasn't even the third.

Levi grunted under his breath and tried the bolt again, his face growing redder with each attempt.

Daniel cleared his throat. "Want me to give that a turn?"

Levi exhaled hard and moved back, running a hand through his thinning gray hair. "It's this blasted thing. Nothing on it makes sense anymore."

Samuel straightened, wiping his hands on a rag, his voice even but careful. "You rebuilt this planter blindfolded just three springs ago."

Levi gave a tight nod but didn't answer.

The silence settled in thickly, broken only by the distant lowing of cows across the pasture. Dust floated in beams of morning light pouring through the slats of the barn wall.

Daniel moved to the planter, gave the bolt a quick twist, and slipped the hitch into place. Easy. Simple. A job Levi could've done in his sleep… before.

He glanced over at his father-in-law, who stood staring at the tool bench but not really seeing it.

And suddenly Daniel knew. That blankness. That slow unraveling of purpose. It was the same hollow ache he saw in Katie's eyes most mornings. The same confusion wrapped in pride. The same silent, bitter grief. He was losing the rhythm of life that Ruth's hands had always kept.

"She used to keep my workbench clean and tidy," Levi abruptly stared into the cluttered mess of strewn tools. "Had a system for everything… I never paid it much mind."

Samuel's mouth tightened. He nodded slowly, jaw working.

"*Mamm* always said you'd lose your head if you didn't keep it tied on with baler twine."

It was meant to lighten the air, but his *datt* didn't smile.

Instead, Levi turned toward the door and grabbed his hat off a nail. "I'm going to walk the field," he muttered. "Nothing needs fixing out there."

They watched him go and the barn felt colder when he left.

Samuel inclined on the workbench, wiping at a stubborn grease stain on his palm. "He's not the same, not since..."

"I know," Daniel replied.

Samuel watched his *datt* as he walked away, and for the first time, the sorrow revealed a man shouldering the slow unraveling of the world as he knew it.

"I don't know how to help him," Samuel admitted. "I don't think he wants it."

Daniel thought of Katie. Of her reserve. Her sharp words and long stretches of staring at the wall. "He doesn't. Not now. But he will eventually."

Samuel nodded. There was nothing else to say.

The two men went back to the planter, tightening bolts and shifting pieces into place, saying little. Because sometimes, for men like them, love was in the work. And grief… grief was in the doing.

***

The house was still except for the quiet shuffle of feet on the floorboards and the occasional creak of the rocking chair as Mary rocked her cloth doll in the corner of the girls' bedroom. Ella sat on the floor near the window, humming as she arranged wooden animals into a crooked circle.

Katie had taken the baby into the bedroom an hour ago, murmuring something about needing to rest. After nursing him, she'd laid Danny in his cradle, then curled up on the bed, her body folding into the mattress like it might swallow her whole.

The heaviness hadn't left her since her mother passed, not in the mornings, not in the night. Sleep was her only refuge now.

Mary walked toward the hallway and peeked into her bedroom. Her *mamm* hadn't moved when she whispered her name. So Mary shut the door quietly and took charge.

Mary stood on a stool, sleeves pushed up, gripping the carving knife in both hands as she carefully sliced the ham their mother had taken from the smokehouse a week ago. Beside her, Ella sat on her knees in a chair, reaching for pickles with sticky fingers. The girls worked in silence, like shadows playing house, pretending everything was fine.

But it wasn't pretend.

Mary had heard the clock chime eleven. Noon was coming fast, and *Datt* would be in for his meal. And *Mamm* still hadn't gotten up.

The ham was slippery. The knife was heavier than she imagined. She adjusted her grip and made another slow cut. The screen door slammed open behind her as her father's boots hit the floorboards hard. He stopped cold.

The color drained from his face. "Mary." His voice was low, sharp, and to the point. "Put it down. Right now."

Mary froze, the knife hovering in midair.

He was across the room in seconds. The blade was out of her hands before she could blink. He slammed it onto the counter with a loud crack that made both girls jump.

"What are you doing?" His voice rose, shaking, not with anger, but with terror. "You don't ever touch this knife. Do you understand me?"

Mary's chin trembled. "I was just trying to help."

"Help?" He spun, voice tight. "Where's your mother?"

"Sleeping." Her voice cracked.

Daniel turned without another word. He took the stairs two at a time, three if he could've managed it, and shoved open the bedroom door so hard it hit the wall behind it.

Katie flinched awake, eyes unfocused.

"It's almost noon. Mary's in the kitchen… on a stool, cutting ham with a carving knife. Because you're still sleeping in the middle of the day!"

Katie sat up, blinking. "Daniel, please—"

"*Nee*!" He ran a hand over his face, trying to contain the fire building in his chest. "You don't get to 'please' me right now. She could've sliced her hand open. Ella could've pulled that stool down on top of her. They're *kinner*, and they're trying to hold this house together because their *mamm* won't get out of bed!"

The baby jolted awake, wailing. Katie scooped him up, her arms clumsy with panic. "I didn't know… I didn't mean…"

"You didn't *see*," he snapped. "It's been over a month. I've tried to be patient. I've tried to give you time. But this… this is dangerous."

Daniel stood in the doorway, chest heaving, eyes blazing

with something that looked like pain disguised as fury.

Katie's tears slipped down her cheeks, silent and hot.

And downstairs, Mary held Ella's hand beneath the table, the two of them listening as the sound of their broken family echoed through the walls. Mary silently wiped a tear from Ella's cheek while trying not to cry herself.

***

Daniel turned from the bedroom before he could see Katie cry. If he stood there a second longer, he was afraid he might say something worse… something he couldn't take back.

The bathroom door clicked loudly behind him. He turned on the cold water, let it run for a moment, then plunged his hands under the stream. The chill bit into his skin.

He cupped the water and splashed his face once. Twice.

Then he gripped the sides of the sink, breathing hard.

He could still see the way Mary looked at him… frozen, wide-eyed, that carving knife trembling in her hand. His own voice echoed in his mind, too sharp, too loud. He hadn't meant to be cruel. He was scared. That's all.

He wiped his face with the towel. "I'm trying," he sighed. "But I don't know what else to do." He needed air.

Downstairs, the girls were still under the table, hushed and small in the wake of what they'd heard. He crouched beside them and opened his arms.

Mary came first, crawling into his lap without a word. Ella followed, clinging to her *schwester* more than to him.

Daniel wrapped his arms around them, holding them close until their little hearts stopped racing.

"I shouldn't have yelled like that. I scared you, didn't I?"

Mary nodded against his chest. Ella's thumb crept back into her mouth.

"I was upset," he brushed her hair back lightly, "but not at you. You were trying to help. I know that. But I need you both to promise something for me." They looked up.

"No more sharp knives. Not unless *Mamm* or I give them to you, okay?"

Mary nodded solemnly. "I just didn't want you to come in hungry."

He swallowed hard. "I know. But next time, I'm just fine with peanut butter and jelly."

Ella perked up. "With honey?"

He chuckled. "You drive a hard bargain."

They made sandwiches together, extra honey for Ella, and Daniel packed them into a basket with apples and two cups of milk. He patted the girls' heads and sent them outside with a blanket to have a picnic in the grass under the big maple tree. As the screen door swung shut behind them, the house grew quiet again.

Daniel stood in the middle of the kitchen, staring at the knife on the counter, and sighed. He couldn't do this alone.

He pulled his hat from the peg and stepped onto the back porch. The breeze carried the smell of drying hay and rising heat. His eyes scanned the lane.

If anyone knew what to do, it would be Betty. He didn't know what he'd say when he reached her door, only that he needed her help again.

***

Katie padded down the stairs slowly, her head cloudy from broken sleep and too many dreams of her *mamm's* voice calling out to her.

She stepped into the kitchen, half-expecting to see Daniel at the table or the girls coloring at the bench. But the space was empty, save for the lingering scent of smoked ham.

Her brow furrowed. She walked to the window over the sink and pulled back the curtain. There… under the maple tree whose leaves were just starting to fall around them, Mary and Ella sat cross-legged on the quilt, their picnic basket open between them, small hands holding sandwiches as they chattered between bites. The sun filtered through the leaves, dappled their heads, and for a brief moment, it looked like nothing was wrong at all.

But Katie knew better. Her eyes drifted back to the kitchen counter, and that's when she saw it. The carving knife.

Her breath caught, and a chill rushed over her skin. Her knees buckled against the rim of the sink as her mind raced. The shame hit first, hard and fast. And then, the nausea followed.

She clutched the edge of the basin and bent over it just as her stomach twisted violently. She heaved until there was nothing left but air and shaking. When it was over, she slid to the floor.

She wrapped her arms around her knees, head resting against the cabinet door, breath coming in broken sobs.

She had failed. Not just in small ways, but in the ways that mattered most. Failed her daughters, who tiptoed through the house as if afraid of their own *mamm*. Failed Daniel, whose silent disappointment pressed heavier with each passing day. Failed herself. And worst of all… failed without her *mamm* there to guide her through this hollow season.

The tears came, but she didn't bother to wipe them away. They slid cold against her skin, her hair damp and tangled across her cheeks. She sat unmoving, her back against the cupboard, knees drawn up beneath her apron.

Strength felt like a distant memory. Hope, a stranger.

She no longer cared about trying or even pretending. The heaviness of the house, the stillness, the unspoken needs… it all pressed down too hard.

In a breath no louder than a thought, she whispered, "I don't want this life. Not like this."

And in that still, stale air of the kitchen, Katie realized she wasn't just weary. She was empty. Lost beneath pain she didn't understand.

***

Daniel's boots scuffed the border of the dirt road as he made his way past the hedgerow, the sun high enough to warm his shoulders but not enough to soften the ache in his heart. Just before the bend in the lane where Willow Bridge Road crossed into the northern part of the district, Betty Troyer's white clapboard house came into view.

It sat atop a gentle rise, framed by a split-rail fence and rows of mums and fading marigolds, their autumn colors muted by the cool morning air. The wide wraparound porch seemed to reach for him with open arms, its rocking chairs perfectly still, its hanging baskets full of trailing ivy and the last of the rust-colored geraniums. Something about the place quieted his heart before he even reached the steps.

As he climbed onto the porch, a scent drifted toward him… inviting, sweet, and familiar. Chocolate chip cookies. For a second, he closed his eyes and let the memory wash over him: Katie, barefoot in the kitchen after a Saturday morning at Yoder's Bakery, flour on her nose, handing him a warm cookie with a smirk and a kiss.

That was before. Before Ruth's diagnosis. Before Katie's spark faded to ash.

He tapped the frame of the screen door moderately.

Betty's voice floated from the back of the house. "Coming!"

She appeared in the hallway moments later, wiping her hands on her apron, a dusting of flour on her cheek and a smear of chocolate near the hem of her apron. She smiled wide, her presence as warm as the cookie-laced air.

"Daniel Miller. If I didn't know better, I'd think you made a detour at the smell of cookies. I know you have a sweet tooth bigger than Yoder's Bakery."

He tried to smile. "You're not wrong."

She motioned him inside. "Sit. They're just out of the oven."

He followed her into the bright kitchen, where a tray of golden cookies cooled on a rack. She poured him a glass of cold milk, set it beside the plate, and waited until he took a bite before sitting across from him.

"Something tells me this isn't about cookies."

Daniel stared at the crumbs on the table. "*Nee*. It's about Katie."

Betty folded her hands in her lap, listening.

He exhaled slowly. "She's... she's not getting better. I thought maybe she just needed time. But today—" His voice caught.

“Mary was on a stool. Cutting ham with a long knife. Trying to make lunch. Katie was upstairs, asleep. She didn’t even know. I lost it. Yelled. Scared her. Scared the girls.”

Betty didn’t flinch. “Daniel, what you’re seeing… it’s depression. Deep sorrow that’s rooted in loss. It doesn’t always look like tears. Sometimes it looks like sleep. Sometimes it looks like silence. And sometimes, like forgetting how to care about the things that used to matter.”

“I don’t know how to help her. I’m trying, but I’m losing her.”

“You’re not losing her. You’re walking beside her. You just don’t know where the path leads yet.”

He looked up, eyes tired. “How long does it last?”

“There’s no chart, no schedule. But it moves if it’s loved through. If it’s carried.”

Daniel rubbed the back of his neck. “And what am I supposed to do in the meantime? I can’t just stop working. I’ve got horses to train, bills to pay. The girls need tending. The house needs keeping. I’m one man.”

Betty nodded, her face softening. “I know you are. And I know you’re tired. But you don’t have to be the only one carrying the whole house on your shoulders.”

He sighed. "I can't ask Emma to do more. Katie's already put the bakery entirely on her. Emma's running herself ragged with the children and trying to keep up the business."

"Then it's a good thing you came here. Because I can help. And I will."

Daniel's voice was low, rough with the strain of holding too much for too long. "I feel like a stranger in my own house, and I don't think she's the same Katie."

"She's still in there. Just buried beneath the grief. But your love will bring her back."

He nodded slowly. "I came to ask if you'd be willing to help. Maybe... maybe come stay for a bit. Help with the *kinner*. Be with Katie when I can't. She trusts you, even if she doesn't show it."

Betty's smile deepened. "I was already planning to ask. I've packed a small bag and a ball of yarn. I figure the Lord doesn't open a door without giving me hands to walk through it."

Relief broke over Daniel's face like water.

"*Denkie*."

"I'll bring the cookies with me. And we'll just start with today. Sometimes that's all a woman needs. One kind voice. One small step." She rose, placing the cookies into a tin.

And for the first time in weeks, Daniel felt like maybe, just maybe, they weren't alone in this after all.

***

Katie still sat curled on the kitchen floor, her back pressed against the cool cabinet. She hadn't moved since coming downstairs to find the house still.

A knock rattled the front door, and she froze.

A voice followed, high-pitched and familiar. "Katie? It's just me, Leona. Thought I'd bring you some of my cranberry bread."

Katie didn't answer. She scooted further back beneath the window, clutching her knees, hoping the screen door would muffle any hint of her presence.

Leona's voice drifted through the screen, clipped and firm. "You're not the first to lose your *mamm*, Katie. Sorrow has its place, but we mustn't let it take root too deep. The Lord expects us to carry on."

Katie pressed her forehead to her knees. She didn't want comfort. Not the kind wrapped in soft rebukes and spiritual clichés. She didn't want more well-meaning voices telling her how to move forward when she still couldn't breathe right.

In the Amish way, grief wasn't borne in solitude. Community surrounded the grieving, made casseroles, and offered kind smiles and persistent reminders of *Gott's* will.

But Katie wasn't ready.

She wasn't angry at Leona. But she wasn't ready.

She waited in silence until she heard the woman's footsteps retreat from the porch with instructions that she'd leave the bread on the porch railing.

Then the back door creaked open. Betty's gentle voice called out from over the kitchen table as she set her bag on the floor and the tin of cookies on the table.

And Katie, still crumpled on the floor, blinked up at the open door, the sweet hint of chocolate rising through her tears.

# CHAPTER 4

Emma wiped her hands on her apron and propped against the counter in the back of Yoder's Bakery. The yeasty warmth of rising dough clung to the air, mixed with the sugary scent of cinnamon rolls baking. Two young girls from the community worked quietly at the prep table, their hands dusted with flour as they shaped pie crusts for the afternoon rush.

Katie's absence still echoed in every corner. Emma had grown used to the peaceful hum of her best friend's voice, the way they'd move around each other like a well-practiced dance. Now, it all fell to Emma, and though she was managing, the pressure of it pressed on her shoulders.

The bell above the front door jingled.

Emma glanced toward the storefront, her heart sinking as she spotted Leona Shetler striding in, her mouth already pursed like she'd just bitten a lemon. Leona wasn't known for her subtlety. With a reputation for giving advice whether it was asked for or not, she had a way of turning well-meaning visits into uncomfortable conversations.

"*Guder Mariye*, Emma," Leona chirped, stepping into the bakery with the confidence of someone who believed they owned the place. "Looks like you're holding up alright without Katie."

Emma forced a smile. "I'm managing."

Leona took a dramatic sniff of the air as if judging the very quality of the cinnamon rolls baking in the oven. "I stopped by to check on you, and to say I visited with Katie just now. Or tried to. Poor thing wouldn't even come to the door."

Emma stiffened, wiping the counter with care.

"It's only been six weeks. She's doing the best she can."

Leona clicked her tongue. "*Jah*, but don't you think it's time she started to come out of it? We all have our trials. My cousin lost her husband and was back to church the next Sunday, baking pies like nothing happened."

Emma turned, the towel still in her hand. "Leona, everyone carries misery differently. And Katie's heart was tied up in her *mamm.* You don't just bounce back from that."

"But she has a family," Leona pressed, stepping closer to the counter. "*Kinner* who need her. A business. A husband. She needs to step up and trust the Lord. There's a fine line between grieving and wallowing."

Emma's voice sharpened, though she kept it low. "She's doing what she can. And we're all doing what we can to give her space. She doesn't need judgment, Leona. She needs grace."

Leona huffed and shifted her weight. "I'm just saying, this community won't hold everything together forever. We help, but there's a time when folks need to help themselves, too."

Emma set the towel down and walked around the counter, planting herself between Leona and the back kitchen. Her expression remained calm, but her eyes were fierce.

"Katie's not a burden. She's a mother who just lost her own. And while the rest of us are busy whispering about how long she's taking to heal, she's doing everything she can to survive another day. If that means she needs more time, we'll give it to her. That's what real community does."

The bakery had fallen completely silent. The young girls at the counter stood still, both watching with wide eyes.

Leona, flustered, clutched her basket closer to her middle. "Well. I suppose I've said enough."

Emma offered a curt nod. "*Jah*, I think you have."

Leona turned on her heel and marched out of the bakery, the

bell above the door jingling behind her like a final word.

Emma stood for a long moment, steadying her breathing. Then she turned back to the girls, her tone softening.

"Let's get those pies in the oven, *jah*?"

***

Later that afternoon, after the last of the *Englisch* tour customers had exited the shop and climbed into their passenger van, Emma flipped the "Closed" sign on the bakery door and locked it. She exhaled deeply, the tension of the long day sitting heavy on her shoulders.

Samuel came in the back door, the familiar creak of the hinge making the children perk up. He paused to ruffle the twins' hair before bending to scoop Cindy out of the enclosed play area they had set up near the back of the bakery. She giggled and clung to his neck.

Emma stood in the doorway, wiping her hands on her apron. Samuel's eyes met hers, and he could see it all… the fatigue, the lingering frustration, the worry.

"You're stretched thin?"

Emma tried to nod, but the movement was slow. "It's not

just the work. I can handle the baking. What's harder is feeling like I'm not doing enough. Like I'm failing Katie somehow."

Samuel tilted his head, waiting.

"She's always been the strong one," Emma alleged. "But now I watch this place lose a little more of her every day. Customers ask where she is. I made a mistake on the sourdough order this morning; Katie never would've missed that. And today, I actually raised my voice to Leona Shetler." She let out a breath.

Samuel moved closer and lightly rubbed her arm. "You're not failing her. You're carrying a load that was meant for two."

Emma moved to the counter to wrap up a pie and a loaf of bread for supper. Her fingers trembled as she tied the string. "Should I ask her to come back to the bakery? Would that help her or hurt her more?"

Samuel considered for a moment. "Daniel's been worried. Said she barely speaks some days. But maybe coming back here, just for a few hours, might give her something stable. Something normal to do to keep her mind occupied."

Emma nodded. "Tomorrow's our off Sunday. Maybe I'll ask them over for a picnic. Let the children play, keep things light. I'll walk over after dinner."

Samuel smiled gently. "That sounds just right."

Emma returned the smile, this one small but honest, and picked up the warm loaf. Whatever tomorrow brought, she'd make more of an effort to show up and support her best friend the best she could.

***

The next afternoon, the Miller family arrived just after two o'clock. Katie pushed the baby stroller across the road, and Mary and Ella ran ahead toward the grassy yard. Daniel carried a basket of drinks and picnic plates to the porch while Katie quietly took a seat in the wooden rocker, pulling a shawl tight around her shoulders despite the mild breeze. She barely offered more than a nod when Emma stepped outside to greet her.

Daniel joined Samuel near the grill, the faint glow of charcoal beginning to smolder as they waited for it to heat. The air smelled faintly of hickory smoke and the freshly mown grass that Samuel had cut the day before.

The *kinner* shrieked and laughed as they chased each other around the side of the house, and for a moment, Emma sat beside Katie, soaking in the moment of calm between the noises of play and the murmur of the men talking near the grill.

Emma glanced at Katie. "It's *goot* to see you out of the *haus*."

Katie shrugged. "Daniel wanted to come. I didn't argue."

They sat for another minute, the rocker creaking under Katie's gentle sway.

A sudden cry rang out. Ella had tripped on a root and scraped her palm. Before either woman could react, Mary darted across the yard, kneeling beside her little *schwester* with calm urgency. She checked the scrape, dusted off Ella's dress, and helped her stand.

Emma smiled faintly. "Mary is becoming quite the little mother's helper. She's grown up fast these last few weeks."

Katie stiffened. "Don't you think I see it?"

Emma blinked, surprised by the sharpness in her tone. She turned her eyes toward the yard. "I didn't mean it like that."

Another long pause followed. Emma reached into her apron pocket and pulled out a folded pamphlet. She hesitated, then held it out to Katie.

"I picked this up at the Mercantile. It's for a new counseling center in Willow Springs. They've also got someone at the family clinic. A midwife to the Amish. Maybe just talking to someone could help."

Katie looked at the paper but didn't take it.

"I don't need to talk to someone."

Emma pressed her lips together. "Sometimes it helps to talk through the parts we can't fix. Even if it's just to breathe a little easier."

Katie stood abruptly, her chair scraping against the porch floor. "I said I'm fine. I don't need a counselor. I just need to get through the day without everyone telling me what I should be doing."

Emma rose as well. "I was just trying to help."

Katie sank back into the chair, folding her arms. Emma hesitated another moment, then turned and walked toward the yard to join the children. Laughter bubbled up from the far side of the fence as Daniel and Samuel tossed a ball to the boys, and Emma glanced back once.

Katie stared out past the porch rail, unmoving.

Emma sighed, then crouched beside Ella to help wipe her scraped hand with a damp cloth. Love still lingered… in the quiet gestures, in the steadiness of the day, but Katie would have to choose when to let it in again.

***

Katie remained in the rocker long after Emma left, her shawl drawn close, fingers knotted in the fringe. Her eyes stayed fixed on a frayed edge of the porch rail, unwilling to lift.

Below, Daniel bent over the grill, Samuel talking easily at his side. Emma moved with easy grace, skirts brushing fallen leaves as she gathered the little ones. Even Ella, her hand bandaged, her cheeks pink, was laughing.

They looked like a family. A whole one.

Katie stared through the porch rail, the slats like silent bars between her and them. Her own kin, and yet... not.

Daniel knelt to fix a shoe, the line of his shoulders easy, familiar. When Mary rushed up with an armful of leaves, he ruffled her hair and smiled, a smooth smile, the kind that used to be hers. A smile she hadn't drawn from him in months.

Her chest tightened.

She sat in the rocker, a part of the scene and apart from it, both at once. From upstairs windows, from shuttered rooms, from beneath heavy quilts, she had been watching life continue without her. Now it played out in front of her, untouchable.

Mary's small hands flashed through her mind, clutching the carving knife, brow furrowed in grown-up concentration. Daniel's harsh voice that day, raw with fear. Emma's gentle urging her to talk to someone was met with her cold refusal.

Shame burned low in her stomach, but she swallowed it down. No tears came now, only a dry, hollow ache.

The sound of children's feet thudded in the grass. Mary squealed, high and clear, as Samuel swung her to his shoulders. The other little ones darted between legs and under branches, the yard alive with motion. At the picnic table beneath the old maple, Betty sat beside Levi, both of them watching the children with weary affection.

Life was happening with or without her.

Her hand gripped the rocker arm tightly, nails digging into worn wood. She should go down. She knew that. But her feet wouldn't move. Her body wouldn't rise. The very thought of stepping into that bright, bustling circle made her cold inside.

She watched through the slats, pulse fluttering low. They would go on with or without her. And if she never found her way back… well, perhaps no one would even notice.

***

Levi sat on one side of the bench, a cup of coffee cradled between his calloused hands. His straw hat lay on the table beside him, and his eyes followed Mary as she darted past with a string of leaves knotted like garland.

He didn't notice Betty approach until she settled down across from him, a jar of lemonade in her hand and her familiar woven basket at her feet.

"You've got *goot* grandchildren, Levi," she gave him a small smile.

He gave a quick nod, his focus never leaving the yard. "Ruth would've liked to see 'em like this."

Betty tilted her head slightly. "She sees more than you think."

Levi huffed softly, his lips twitching like he wanted to argue, but didn't quite have the strength.

After a moment, he spoke. "I'm grateful you've been helping with Katie. Daniel says it's made a difference, even if she don't say much."

"I don't expect her to say much yet," Betty replied. "Grief clogs the throat something fierce. But I've seen her look at those children like she's still in there. That's something."

Levi ran his thumb along the rim of his mug. "It's been well over a month. Feels like yesterday. Feels like ten years ago. I can't tell which most days."

"That's loss for you." Betty looked out across the yard. "It warps time. And everything else."

He turned to look at her then… really looked. Her eyes were balanced, framed by fine lines of age and sorrow and knowing.

"You lost your *mun* almost twelve years ago, didn't you?"

She nodded. "Heart failure. Wasn't a shock to the doctor, but it sure was to me."

Levi didn't answer right away. His fingers tightened around his cup.

"I still sleep on one side of the bed," he muttered, more to himself than her. "Can't bring myself to move over. And every morning I go to the shed, I expect to find her standing in the garden."

"You don't have to stop missing her, Levi, you just have to keep living while you do."

He blinked hard before he replied, "Don't know that I'm doing much of that either."

"You are… you're helping Samuel with the horses. You're showing up here today. And you let me step in when your family needed another pair of hands."

He shook his head slowly. "We shouldn't need the help."

Betty smiled, but it wasn't patronizing. "No one walks through loss without leaning on someone. Not even the stubborn ones."

Levi gave a throaty chuckle at that, a low, gravelly sound that surprised them both.

They sat in companionable silence for a while, listening to life play out around them.

Betty let out a small breath. "There'll come a day when Ruth's memory won't feel like a blade. More like a blanket. Warm. Worn. And soft enough to carry."

Levi didn't answer. He just nodded.

***

The wafting aroma of grilled hot dogs and warm cider lingered in the air. Emma wiped her hands on her apron and walked slowly up to the porch.

Katie hadn't moved much, her eyes fixed somewhere beyond the perimeter of the yard, lost in her own thoughts as she nursed Danny.

Emma kept her voice gentle. "Supper's ready. Thought

maybe you'd like to come sit with us."

Katie hesitated, but she gave a slow nod and pushed herself up.

The short walk to the picnic table felt longer than it should have, and by the time she sat down between Daniel and Emma, the energy had already shifted.

Samuel handed her a plate with a hot dog and a scoop of potato salad. "The kids helped with the pickles," he offered with a grin, clearly trying.

Katie murmured a *denkie*, barely loud enough to hear.

The conversation moved around her. Emma talked about the new girls she'd hired to help roll pie dough, and Samuel teased her about overbaking the sourdough again. Katie gave a few small smiles, nods where needed, but the quietness between her words stretched longer than the sentences themselves.

Daniel gently bounced Danny over his shoulder, but the baby's fussiness had grown into a wail, and it only added to the heaviness around the table.

Katie flinched as the baby's cries rose in pitch. Her shoulders tensed, her grip on the fork tightening. She turned her face away slightly, but not fast enough for Betty to miss it.

Betty reached over, pushing her paper plate aside. "I'll take him," she offered with a loving smile. "He and I are already old friends."

Daniel passed the baby over with a grateful sigh. Betty rose and cradled him against her shoulder, patting his bottom and calming him. "Why don't you stay and visit a while?" she added softly, with a glance toward Katie. "You need a moment without a crying babe in your arms."

Katie didn't answer, but she didn't leave either.

Levi stood then, announcing that he should be heading home as well. With a wave and a small tip of his hat, he crossed the yard and disappeared into his *haus*.

Samuel stood and clapped Daniel on the shoulder. "Check on those new horses before we call it a day?"

Daniel rose from the bench. "*Jah*."

Emma scooted a little closer to Katie, who was now sitting stiffly, picking at her food with more interest in her spoon than her supper.

They sat in silence for a few moments.

Then Emma broke it. "I've been thinking… maybe you'd consider coming back to the bakery. Just for an hour or two, if you feel up to it."

Katie froze.

Emma pressed on, her tone silky. "You wouldn't have to do much. Just sit and roll pie crust, or help prep the apple fillings. You always liked that."

Katie shook her head quickly. "I'm not ready."

"I know, I just… I miss you. And so does the bakery. It's not the same without your humming in the kitchen and your way of getting that perfect crimp on every pie."

She smiled, trying to lighten the air between them.

Katie blinked quickly and looked down at her lap.

"I forgot to tell you," Emma added with a chuckle, "I ruined two dozen oatmeal raisin cookies last week because I used salt instead of sugar. Not sure what made me try a bite of a broken cookie… but I'm so glad I did!"

Katie's lips twitched, and for a second, the corner of her mouth curled up. "You always hated oatmeal raisin," she muttered.

Emma laughed softly. "Still do."

A breeze rustled through the trees above them.

"I'm not saying yes, but I'll think about it."

"That's all I'm asking."

Emma leaned over and gave her arm a light squeeze. "With Betty staying with you, she can take care of the girls in the mornings for a while. Maybe that was *Gott's* way of making space for you to take a breath."

Katie didn't respond, but she didn't pull away either.

As the sky deepened into the lavender hues of dusk, the two women sat side by side, quiet, but together.

# CHAPTER 5

The morning sun had barely broken over the treetops when the kitchen filled with the clatter of dishes. Betty had already taken the girls out to gather eggs, their small voices echoing from the chicken coop beyond the barn. The baby napped upstairs in the cradle by the window, and for the first time that week, the house was hushed.

Katie stood at the sink, staring out into the golden October haze, her hands resting on the rim of the counter. She hadn't moved in several minutes, not since Daniel walked in with that tightness in his shoulders she knew too well.

He set the bucket of wood by the stove and wiped his hands on his trousers. "We need to talk."

She didn't turn.

"Can we not do this now?" Her voice was flat.

Daniel lowered his voice, glancing toward the open window. "Betty's outside with the girls. They won't hear us."

"I don't want to talk."

"Well, I do."

That got her attention. She turned slowly, her face pale and her hair peeking out from underneath her dingy *kapp*, which spoke more of weariness than effort.

Daniel rubbed a hand over his face. "You need to go talk to someone."

Her expression hardened. "What for and have you been talking to Emma?"

"You know what for." He lowered his voice further, but the edge in it remained. "You don't get out of bed some days. You don't eat. You won't hold the baby unless someone hands him to you. The girls are—" he caught himself. "They need their *mamm*. And I need my *fraa*."

"I'm doing the best I can."

"*Nee*, you're not." His voice was a little sharper than he intended. "You're barely doing anything. And I'm sorry, but I can't keep pretending that's okay."

Katie's jaw clenched. "You think I don't know what I've become? I live inside this every second of the day. I don't need some doctor to confirm that I'm a failure."

"You're not a failure."

"I feel like one."

Daniel paced a short circle, the wood floor creaking beneath his boots. He stopped in front of her and dropped his voice to a whisper. "I don't care if it's a doctor, a bishop, or Betty herself. You need to talk to someone. Because if something doesn't change, this house is going to break under the strain."

No tears welled in Katie's eyes; her face was stone.

Daniel's frustration boiled over. "You're pulling this whole family down with you," he gritted his teeth. "So either find a way to help… or else I'll be finding someone for you."

The words hung in the air like smoke after a firecracker. Not a threat, not really, but a line.

He didn't wait for her reply. His boots struck the floor in heavy steps as he stormed out the back door, letting it slap shut behind him.

Katie stood in the hush that followed, the silence pressing heavier than Daniel's words. The door had barely clicked shut, but it echoed in her chest like a slammed gate.

Outside, her daughters' laughter floated up, high, sweet, and untethered. The porch swing creaked in slow rhythm, Betty's calm voice threading through the stillness like a hymn Katie couldn't quite join.

She gripped the edge of the counter.

He was right. She hated how true it felt. But knowing she had to try and knowing how were two very different burdens.

Her eyes landed on the cluttered sink. Half-washed dishes, hardened bits of oatmeal, remnants of a busy kitchen. Everything looked exactly like she felt, abandoned in place.

She reached for the faucet and twisted the handle hard. Hot water rushed out, steaming instantly. The first plate she picked up slipped in her grasp, clattering back into the basin and splashing water onto her dress. She didn't flinch.

She scrubbed harder.

Not because she believed the chore would fix anything… But because doing nothing was starting to ache more than the doing.

Her hands moved automatically, scrubbing with a force that bordered on anger. Grief had taken everything from her… her mother, her spark, her footing as a wife and mother. She hadn't realized how far she'd drifted until Daniel said it out loud.

The creak of the swing, the giggles outside, the scent of warm bread cooling on the table… life was happening. Still happening. Even without her.

Katie pressed the plate against the rag with trembling fingers, then paused mid-motion.

"I don't know how," she whispered, voice barely audible. "But I want to."

The words weren't for anyone but the quiet kitchen… a confession sent up like steam from the full basin. She swallowed hard and kept washing.

***

Katie didn't know why she turned toward her parents' *haus* that afternoon. Maybe it was the gravity of Daniel's words still sitting heavy on her chest, or the way the kitchen felt too full with Betty's gentle humming and the girls playing underfoot. She just… needed air. Space.

The back door of her childhood home creaked on its hinges as she pushed it open. The familiar scuff of the mat, the smell of lemon oil and faint pipe tobacco, it all felt frozen in time, as if her mother might step into the kitchen at any moment, flour on her apron and kindness in her eyes.

But the room was quiet. Empty.

Until she spotted her father sitting at the kitchen table,

glasses perched low on his nose, reading *The Budget* newspaper, its creased pages open wide.

Levi looked up, surprised.

"Katie."

"*Datt.*"

She hesitated in the doorway, suddenly feeling like a child again, unsure if she belonged.

He folded the paper in half and gestured to the chair across from him. "Coffee's still warm on the stove if you want some."

She moved slowly across the kitchen and poured herself a half cup, her hands trembling slightly as she sat down at the table. The mug was one of her mother's, blue with a tiny chip at the rim.

"I haven't been back since…"

"You boxed up her things."

Katie nodded, staring into her coffee. "Feels wrong being here without her."

Levi tipped back in his chair, the wood creaking beneath his weight. "Every morning I still expect to hear her fussing with the stove or hollering at me for tracking in mud. But the Lord took her home. That's the part that don't change."

Katie swallowed hard. "I don't know how to move on."

He nodded slowly, looking out the window for a long moment before speaking. "I've been stuck in my own way too. Just… quieter about it, I suppose."

She glanced at him.

"You think I haven't sat in this chair at night asking *Gott* why He took her so soon?" he continued. "She was the glue in this family. But wallowing in misery? That ain't what your mother would want. And you know it."

Katie's lip quivered. "I just miss her so much."

"I know." He reached across the table and laid his calloused hand over hers. "But she'd be real disappointed if she thought her passing took you with her."

Katie looked down, blinking hard.

"Your *kinner* still need their *mamm*. Daniel needs his *fraa*. And me…" His voice grew tender. "I need my *dochder*."

A tear slipped down her cheek.

"She'd be the first one telling you to get out of bed, comb your hair, and face the day. Even if it's hard… especially when it's hard."

Katie managed a tiny, tearful laugh. "She would've handed me a broom and told me to stop feeling sorry for myself."

"That she would."

They were quiet for a moment.

Then Levi looked at her more firmly. "Don't wait until the *kinner* are grown and gone to wish you'd been present. This time, it doesn't come back."

Guilt stung at her. She hadn't once asked how her *datt* was doing. She'd been so consumed in her own pain that she'd forgotten he'd lost the love of his life.

"I'm sorry I haven't checked in on you more."

He waved the apology away. "We all grieve differently. But don't let it turn into a habit."

She nodded, eyes glassy but more focused than they'd been in weeks.

Levi picked up his cup. "She used to say, 'Life's for the living.' She meant it, too."

Katie looked down at the old mug again.

Maybe it was the memory of home. The warm coffee. The silence that didn't need fixing. Or maybe it was hearing her mother's words through her father's mouth that did it.

But something shifted. She wasn't whole. She wasn't ready.

But she was still here… trying to pull herself together one way or another.

***

Dark clouds moved in quickly as Katie stood at the sink rinsing a bowl of apples, her hands working in perfect rhythm. She hadn't said much since returning home from her father's, but something in the way she moved, slower, more focused, told Betty a change was coming.

Betty wiped her hands on her apron and leaned against the counter, watching the younger woman with quiet intent.

"You had a good visit with your *datt*?"

Katie gave a small nod, setting an apple aside and reaching for another. A pause stretched between them, comfortable but waiting. Then Katie's voice came, barely louder than the trickle of the tap. "I don't think I can keep pretending I've got it all under control."

Betty looked up, her eyes softening. "No one expects you to."

Katie turned off the water and braced her hands on the sink edge, her shoulders trembling just slightly. "I've been trying to outrun this. But I can't. And now it's catching up."

Betty walked closer, resting a hand on her arm. "That right there… that's the first honest thing you've said in weeks."

Katie looked at her, eyes rimmed red. "What if I don't know how to fix it?"

"You don't need to fix it." Betty's voice was kind but firm. "You need to feel it. And then you need to let someone walk beside you while you figure out what comes next."

Katie blinked. "You told me it'd come… when I was ready."

Betty smiled, a knowing smile that only comes with miles of life behind it. "And here you are."

Katie let out an easy laugh through her tears, surprised at how light she felt just saying it aloud.

"I don't even know where to begin."

"Well," Betty pulled a stool from under the counter and patting it. "Sit yourself down, and we'll start small. First thing is sunshine. Every day. Even if it's just to sit on the porch for ten minutes with a hot mug of tea, you need fresh air and sunshine."

Katie sat, pulling her sweater around her. "I can do that."

"Second thing." Betty opened the cupboard and started rummaging, "less sugar for a little while. Sugar plays tricks with your moods, especially when you're already low. We'll focus on fresh fruit, vegetables, and protein for now. It'll help."

Katie sighed, but a tiny smile tugged at the corner of her mouth. "So… no cinnamon rolls?"

"Not for a bit. But when you're stronger, then perhaps you can enjoy them again."

Katie nodded. "That sounds nice."

Betty pulled up her own stool beside her. "And third, and maybe most important, we talk. Every day. Just for a few minutes, even if it's about the weather or how many eggs the hens gave us. Talking keeps the fog from settling back in."

Katie looked down at her hands. "What stage is this again?"

Betty tilted her head. "Bargaining. It's where your heart starts whispering, *What if I try? What if I change this one thing? What if it helps?* It's a turning place, not an ending, but a choice."

Katie let that settle beneath her breastbone. "So what comes after that?"

Betty's smile softened. "We'll deal with that when it comes… and it will come for *sure and certain*."

A long silence settled between them before Katie spoke again. "You think I'll ever feel like myself again?"

Betty placed her hand lightly over hers. "No, Katie-girl. You'll never be the same. But that doesn't mean you won't be whole. You'll be someone new. Someone stronger. Someone who still carries your mother in your heart… right where she belongs."

***

Supper had come and gone, dishes stacked in the basin, leftovers covered in the refrigerator. Betty had taken the baby upstairs for his evening bath, her sweet voice humming a lullaby that hadn't been sung in years. The girls had finished their evening chores and were sitting on the braided rug, one with a picture book, the other threading buttons onto string.

Katie sat on the front steps, her arms wrapped around her knees, her sweater pulled tightly against the October chill. The faint trace of wood smoke drifted in the air, mingling with the faint sweetness of apples from the bins by the shed.

She hadn't cried after Daniel left that morning. She hadn't done much of anything. Just sat. And listened to the quiet weight of her life.

The door creaked behind her. She didn't turn, assuming it was Betty, but then came the soft padding of tiny bare feet and the small voice that rarely came with a demand.

"*Mamm*?"

Katie blinked and looked over her shoulder. Mary stood holding a folded blanket and a half-finished doll, her thumb resting on her bottom lip.

"*Jah*?"

Mary hesitated, then crossed to the step and sat beside her. She placed the blanket across both their laps and snuggled close, her warmth a subtle comfort Katie didn't realize she needed.

"*Grossmommi* Ruth used to say the moon was *Gott's* nightlight so we wouldn't be afraid in the dark."

Katie's breath caught, a low ache rising in her throat. "Did she?"

Mary nodded. "She said even if we can't see Him, He still sees us. Just like the moon."

Katie looked up, and sure enough, the moon had started its slow rise above the treetops… silver and steady against the darkening sky.

"I miss her," Mary whispered. "Sometimes when I miss her, I smell cinnamon. Like her oatmeal."

Katie swallowed hard, her voice barely a whisper. "I miss her too."

They sat in silence, the kind only children and grieving mothers can share.

Then Mary looked up at her. “Remember when she taught us how to make apple dumplings and I tipped the whole tub of flour on the floor? You laughed so hard.”

Katie’s lip trembled. She hadn’t thought of that moment in months. Her *mamm* had stood behind Mary, guiding her hands to roll the dough just right. Katie had been sitting across the table, watching them. That day, her mother had looked at her with a light in her eyes that said, “*This is what memories are made of.*”

Katie had laughed then, real laughter, bright, unguarded, full.

And now, as the memory surfaced, it was like a warm quilt from a cedar chest covering them with the sweetness of a time gone by.

Mary burrowed into her side. “Maybe you could show me how to make them like she did. You said once we’d make them again.”

Katie pressed a kiss into the top of her daughter’s tiny *kapp* and whispered, “I’d like that.”

The door creaked again, and this time it was Betty, holding

a warm mug of tea for her. She didn't say anything, just handed it over, her eyes taking in the moment and adding nothing to it but presence.

After Mary headed back inside with her doll, Katie stayed on the porch. The moon continued to rise, casting long silver shadows across the back fields.

For the first time in weeks, Katie didn't feel like she had to run from the quiet. She let the tea warm her fingers. She let the ache sit beside her instead of swallowing her whole.

And she let the memory of her mother, flour-covered and laughing, stay a little longer than it had the day before.

***

It was late by the time Daniel returned home. The lantern on the porch had long gone out, the hearth fire inside just glowing embers. He slipped in through the mudroom, careful not to let the screen door bang shut behind him. The house was silent, the kind of deep peace that meant everyone was finally asleep.

He moved through the kitchen in practiced calm, the subtle note of Betty's evening baking still clinging to the air, molasses cookies, maybe. His boots were dusted with the red clay of Sugarcreek and the sour scent of horse sweat still lingered on his shirt. It had been a long day.

The trip had taken more out of him than he'd expected. Two new horses were now in his care, green and full of skittish energy. But it wasn't the training that tired him.

It was the state of his home that weighed him down.

He climbed the stairs slowly, the familiar creaks of the wood greeting him like old companions. He paused at the girl's door, cracked open just an inch, and listened to the steady rhythm of their breathing. A comfort.

He pushed open the door to the bedroom and stood there for a moment, letting his eyes adjust to the moonlight filtering through the window. Katie lay on her side, her back to him. The quilt rose and fell in slow, even breaths.

He changed quietly, moving with the reverence of a man who didn't want to wake what peace might finally be present in the room. Slipping beneath the covers, he tried not to shift too much, letting the cool sheets settle around him.

Just as he closed his eyes, he felt it.

Her hand. Sliding across the space between them, fingers curling against his shirt, gripping the fabric lightly, like someone reaching out in the dark for a tether.

He opened his eyes, heart thudding in the stillness.

She didn't say a word.

Neither did he.

He rolled onto his side, pulling her into his arms without question, without needing to ask. She came easily, pressing her face against his chest, her breath moist through his thin nightshirt.

They held each other, wrapped in silence, in ache, in fragile understanding.

Daniel didn't know if anything had truly changed. Sorrow had no calendar, no deadline. But for the first time in two months, she had reached for him. And that, he knew, was something.

He closed his eyes and let the rhythm of her breathing guide him to sleep, hope resting discreetly between them in the dark.

# CHAPTER 6

The clang of the empty cup hitting the floor echoed through the kitchen louder than it should have.

"Ella, I said to carry the cup to this sink, not drop it on the floor. Look at the mess you've made!"

Katie gritted her teeth as Ella burst into tears. She didn't even mean to shout, but the sharpness in her voice had cut clean through the morning stillness like a knife. She bent to pick up the cup, her knuckles white, her chest tight with irritation.

"It was just an accident," Betty crouched beside Ella and brushed her tears away with the hem of her apron.

Katie didn't respond. She couldn't.

From the corner of her eye, she caught Mary hovering in the doorway, holding baby Daniel on her hip with the practiced ease of someone far older than five. When their eyes met, Mary looked away.

The knot in Katie's stomach twisted tighter, and she turned

back to the sink, scrubbing the breakfast dishes with a force that left suds splashing up her arms. Betty gathered the girls and ushered them into the front room, her calm voice low and soothing, offering them a story and some fresh apple slices.

Katie's throat burned. Not from tears. From shame. From fury. From the unfairness of it all.

She was their *mamm*. Why were they constantly crawling into Betty's lap for comfort?

"Girls," she called over her shoulder, sharper than intended, "pick up your toys before *Datt* comes in for dinner."

No answer. Just the creak of the rocking chair as Betty settled in, followed by her quiet hum of an old lullaby she used to sing.

Daniel stepped inside just then, the smell of the horse barn clinging to his jacket. He paused just inside the door, taking in the room, Katie at the sink, stiff with tension; Betty rocking with the girls, the strained calm. He walked slowly to the counter and poured himself a mug of coffee.

"You alright?" His voice was low, careful.

Katie didn't look at him. "Fine."

Daniel nodded once, but his eyes lingered on the living room.

"They've been going to Betty more lately."

Katie's jaw clenched. "They're just *kinner*. They don't understand." Her tone was clipped, defensive.

"I know." He took a sip, watching her over the rim of his mug. "But they miss you."

"I'm right here." Her voice cracked… not from tears, but from sheer exasperation. "I haven't gone anywhere."

He nodded again, but she saw it. That look. The one that said *yes, you have*.

Katie turned back to the sink, blinking hard. The rage simmered low, pressing beneath her breast. She was angry at the dishes, at the cup, at the way Daniel looked at her like she was broken. Angry at her children for needing more than she had to give. And angry… perhaps most of all at herself.

She set the last plate in the rack and wiped her hands slowly. Daniel was already walking toward the front room, drawn to the tender sounds of his children laughing at one of Betty's stories.

She watched him go and hated the jealousy that was trapped in her breath. They should be in her lap, not Betty's.

***

Daniel paused on the threshold between the kitchen and front room, watching Betty finish braiding Ella's hair while Mary stacked blocks in the corner. The girls looked calm now, safe, but the earlier tension still weighed on him.

Betty caught his eye and gave a small, knowing nod. She sent the girls off to gather crayons and scrap paper.

Daniel sat heavily on the edge of the settee, rubbing his hands together, not from the cold but to settle his nerves.

"She snapped at Ella again," she murmured. "Over nothing." She shook her head. "It scared them both." Betty folded her hands and crossed her knees. "But it wasn't about the cup."

"I know." He leaned forward, elbows on knees. "It's everything. It's depression, it's her body not being right... it's the pull of trying to hold on when she's too tired to." He let out a breath. "But I'm learning something. No matter how patient I try to be, she can't pull out of this on her own."

Betty gave a quiet nod. "*Nee*. She won't. Not yet."

Daniel looked toward the kitchen. His voice was low but certain. "Then I have to stop walking on eggshells. It's not helping her. Or the girls. Or me." His jaw tightened. "If she's going to come back to us, she needs a reason. And someone willing to pull her back when she can't see the way."

For the first time in weeks, his voice didn't waver or sag under the weight of everything. It stood firm, clear and sure.

Betty studied him a moment. "A husband's strength is a gift. But so is wisdom in knowing when to push... and when to sit quietly beside her."

He nodded. "I know. But today... today, she's coming outside. If for no other reason than to remember there's still a world waiting."

Betty smiled. "I'll keep the girls here."

Daniel rose, shoulders squared. He found Katie in the mudroom, pulling wood for the stove, her shawl already wrapped tight.

"Come outside with me."

She blinked at him. "It's cold."

"You need the cold air."

Before she could argue, he opened the door. The screen creaked and banged shut behind them as Katie marched out. The gray November sky hung heavy. Wind tugged at her shawl, the chill sharp on her cheeks.

Daniel stood by the porch railing, eyes scanning the fields. He didn't speak at first. Just breathed, hands loose at his sides.

Katie settled stiffly into the rocker.

Daniel's voice broke the tension. "We can't keep going like this. Your emotions are up and down, and we don't ever know what version of you we're going to get."

She stared ahead and didn't answer.

He exhaled hard. "I know you're hurting. I know this isn't what you asked for. But none of us did." His tone was firm but no longer bitter. Just weary truth. "You're still their *mamm*. And you're still my *fraa*. And I can't stand by while this pain steals more from us than it already has."

Her voice came sharply. "I didn't ask you to stand by."

Daniel shook his head, quiet for a long beat. Then, softer, but stable: "I know. But I made vows to stand beside you anyway."

He turned toward the steps. "I'm going to town. I'll eat there." He hesitated, then added, voice gentler. "Think about this, Katie. For your sake. For theirs. It's time you got some help."

Without waiting for an answer, he left her on the porch, boots crunching on the gravel drive.

This time, the door stayed shut. No angry exit. Just a man standing still, ready to fight for his family, even if the fight would take longer than he'd hoped.

***

The buggy wheels crunched along the gravel lane as the wind whipped through the almost bare trees. Daniel guided the horse with a loose grip, reins limp in his hands. He hadn't meant to end up at Bishop Schrock's, but somehow the horse knew the way. Or maybe *Gott* did.

Light spilled from the bishop's kitchen window as Daniel slowed the mare, climbed down, and tied her at the hitching post. He crossed the yard with heavy, dragging steps, each one stirring the damp earth beneath him. At the porch, he raised his hand and knocked on the screen door, his knuckles brushing the wood like it might splinter.

Moments later, Bishop Schrock opened it, his suspenders relaxed over a faded white shirt, still smelling faintly of a day's hard work.

"Daniel," he exclaimed with calm surprise. "This is a pleasant surprise."

Daniel removed his hat and held it at his side.

"I... I didn't know where else to go."

The bishop nodded once and moved aside.

"Then you came to the right place."

Inside, the kitchen smelled of roasted chicken and fresh-baked bread. Bishop Schrock gestured for him to sit at the table, where a Bible and a pair of reading glasses lay open beside a cooling mug of tea.

Daniel dropped onto a chair, shoulders slumping as a long, ragged breath slipped from his chest, slow and shaky, like it had clawed its way out after being buried too long.

"It's Katie. I've tried to help her through the loss of her *mamm*. I've tried patience, silence, work, prayer... but it feels like she's stuck, and I'm watching my family fall apart with her."

The bishop folded his hands and listened.

"She's angry now," Daniel went on. "Snapping at the girls. Pulling away from me. And I'm angry too, ashamed to say it, but I'm at my wits' end. I'm worn down trying to be everything for everyone."

"You've taken all that weight onto your shoulders," he paused before continuing, "and you're forgetting who your help comes from."

Daniel's eyes dropped.

"I'm the head of my household. I thought that meant I had to hold everything together."

"It means you lead by example, *jah*, but not by white knuckling your way through. Even our Savior wept. And even He ran to His Father when the burden was too great."

Daniel rubbed his eyes with calloused fingers. "I've yelled more than I've prayed lately."

The bishop didn't scold. "Honesty is a good place to start. It's easy to expect your *fraa* to heal on your timeline, but the Lord works differently in each heart."

"So what do I do?"

"Stay steady. Show her gentleness, even when she bristles. And don't forget, grief turns into anger when it has no place to go. Give her small places to set it down. Don't demand she be the wife she was before, invite her to become the woman *Gott* is shaping her into now."

Daniel leaned back, exhaling hard. "That sounds good. But it's hard when all she does is shut me out."

"Keep showing up anyway. A husband's love isn't measured in ease, it's tested in endurance."

Time hung between them for a few moments.

"She's crushed," Daniel sighed. "And I've been stomping around like she's doing it on purpose."

The bishop rose to pour another mug of tea and set it down

in front of him.

"Your job right now isn't to fix her. It's to walk beside her. Even when she walks too slow."

Daniel nodded, wrapping both hands around the warm mug. "*Dankie,* I needed to hear that."

***

The farmhouse was dark by the time Daniel returned, the lamps turned down low and the only light coming from the kitchen, where Betty had left a covered plate on the table. He didn't have the appetite to lift the towel and see what she'd made.

His boots sat by the door, his coat hung on the peg. Warmth clung to the walls, the scent of home still lingering in the air, but instead of comfort, it pressed against his chest, quiet and hollow, echoing the distance that still stretched between him and Katie.

He paused at the bottom of the stairs and listened. Danny's hungry cries told him she was still awake. He took the steps slowly, the bishop's words firm in his ears.

The bedroom door was half-cracked, lamplight glowing

inside. Katie sat in bed with her back to him, nursing the baby. The muffled sounds of sucking and the rustle of the quilt were the only sounds in the room.

He stepped in and softly closed the door behind him.

She didn't turn.

"I stopped by Bishop Schrock's."

Still nothing.

He moved around to his side of the bed, hesitating before he sat down.

"I asked him what to do… how to help you."

Her shoulders stiffened, then relaxed again. She shifted the baby but still didn't meet his eyes.

"I'm not your project, Daniel."

His heart pinched.

"That's not what I meant."

"Feels like it." Her voice was flat, but there was sharpness underneath.

He waited a beat before trying again. "I know I've said the wrong things… done the wrong things. But I'm trying."

Katie finally looked up. Her eyes were tired. "I don't need you to try. I just need to be left alone."

The words sliced through the space between them.

Daniel nodded slowly and stood. He pulled his pillow from the bed and a blanket from the back of the rocking chair. For a second, he lingered, hoping, maybe, she'd call him back.

But she didn't. He left the room in silence, careful not to let the door creak on his way out.

The kitchen was cool, the warmth from earlier already fading. He laid the pillow on the narrow daybed in the corner, spread the blanket over it, and sat down on the edge. The clock ticked loudly in the stillness.

He slanted forward, elbows on knees, and dropped his head into his hands.

*"Walk beside her. Even when she walks too slow."*

But tonight, she seemed rooted in place, unmoving, and he couldn't shake the ache in his legs, or the weight in his chest, as he wondered how much farther he could go alone.

Still, he pulled the blanket over himself and whispered a prayer. Not for healing, or understanding, or even comfort. Just for endurance.

***

The baby nursed quietly, tucked into the crook of Katie's arm. Her bedroom was dim, the soft rhythm of his sucking the only sound. The house had long since settled for the night. But Katie had not.

She traced small circles along the baby's back, her mind turning as restlessly as the wind tapping against the windowpane.

Across the room, the big bed stood empty on one side. He hadn't come to bed the night before. Or the one before that.

The ache she thought had dulled stirred fresh again.

She pressed a kiss to Danny's downy head, breathing in the sweet scent of soap and milk. "Your *datt* deserves better," she whispered, voice barely a breath in the stillness.

Her gaze drifted to the old wooden cradle by the wall. The one her *mamm* had rocked her in, long before Katie became a mother herself.

For a moment, she could hear her *mamm's* soft humming, picture her gentle hands smoothing covers over a restless babe. There had been no sharp words. No distance. Just love, calm and sure.

A lump rose in Katie's throat. *I can't keep living like this.*

The thought came sudden and unbidden, clear as if spoken aloud.

Not for herself. Not just for Daniel. But for this child in her arms, and the little girls who tiptoed through their days.

When the baby finished, she tucked him gently into the bassinet. A line of moonlight touched the floorboards, pale and thin.

Katie lingered a moment longer, her fingers resting lightly on the edge of the cradle.

Tomorrow…Tomorrow she would try.

Not for perfection. Not for sudden joy. But for one small step back toward her family.

She crossed the room to the dresser where she'd left the day's mail, a habit she hadn't had the strength for in weeks. Most days, she just tossed it aside. But something made her pause tonight.

She thumbed through the stack.

A catalog from *The Fabric Haus*. A folded issue of *The Budget*. A hand-addressed envelope with no return name, only a postmark from Pittsburgh.

She hesitated. The handwriting was unfamiliar. Curled and slanted, the kind of penmanship that belonged to someone who'd taken their time. Curiosity tugged at her.

She tore it open slowly, careful not to wake the baby. Inside was a single sheet of paper and a small clipping from *The Willow Springs Gazette*, a memorial mention of Ruth's passing.

*Dear Mrs. Miller,*

*I hope you don't mind me writing. I met your mother, Ruth, at the Cancer Clinic. We shared a morning in the waiting room. She spoke of you with such love... and such faith.*

*After she passed, one of the nurses told me, and I felt led to reach out. Your mother's strength was a light to me in a very dark time. I just wanted you to know she made a difference, even to strangers.*

*I still remember the way she'd hum hymns under her breath, and how she told me: "Even when the Lord feels far, He's never more than a whisper away."*

*May His nearness comfort you now.*

*In Christ's love,*

*A friend from the waiting room*

Katie read the letter twice. By the third time, her vision blurred, but not just from tears. Frustration welled just beneath the surface, sharp and bitter, like an old wound rubbed raw.

She pressed the paper to her chest, fingers trembling. The handwriting wasn't her *mamm's*, but something about the way the words curved, the cadence, the Scripture, the soft urging toward joy, it felt like her.

Too much like her.

She sat down hard on the edge of the bed, the mattress dipping under her weight. Her pulse thudded in her ears, angry and confused all at once. Her mother's voice seemed to echo faintly, not loud or warm, but haunting.

*He's never more than a whisper away.*

Katie flinched, swiping at her eyes.

"Don't do that," she muttered to the empty room, voice jagged. "Don't sound like her. Don't say the things I need to hear and pretend like they're enough."

The ache in her chest shifted, still there, but no longer clenched tight. Something inside eased, just enough to breathe. But the space it left behind lay bare and tender, as if even the quiet might bruise it.

She crumpled the edge of the letter without meaning to, then smoothed it quickly, as if the creases were a betrayal. Her gaze drifted to the window where the trees swayed gently in the dark.

*How dare this stranger write to me like she knows me.*

And yet...

The letter still sat in her lap. Not torn. Not thrown away.

Katie stared at it for a long time. Long enough for the room to fade into shadows and the weight of the day to settle over her shoulders like a too-heavy quilt.

She wasn't ready to say it aloud, but the thought came anyway.

*Maybe... just maybe... I'm not as alone as I thought.*

She folded the letter, carefully this time, and tucked it beneath her Bible—not to hide it, but to keep it close.

# CHAPTER 7

The sweet smell of cinnamon and nutmeg curled through the air as Katie stepped through the bakery door. It was warm inside, but not just from the ovens. The laughter of young girls behind the counter, the rhythmic clinking of metal trays, and the low murmur of Emma giving instructions all spoke of life continuing without her.

Katie set her basket down slowly, her eyes adjusting to the bright lights after the dull gray of the November morning. She hadn't worn a bonnet, just a scarf, and even that felt too heavy today.

Emma looked up from shaping loaves. Her smile was hesitant, hopeful. "You made it."

"I said I would." Katie moved stiffly toward the sink to wash her hands.

Emma didn't press. She only nodded and pointed toward the prep table. "We've got pumpkin pies and sugar cookies today.

Holiday orders are coming in fast."

Two neighbor girls, likely around sixteen, were rolling pie dough and laughing. One of them looked at Katie shyly and offered a "*Hallo*," before returning to her task.

Katie stood beside Emma, watching a moment too long before following her lead. Her hands moved, but her thoughts wandered. Everything around her was in its place, neat rows, clear labels, Emma's quiet efficiency, but it was as if she'd stepped into a house prepared for someone else. The air was too still, the light too bright, the silence too deep. Nothing had changed… and yet everything had.

The first batch of pies went in the oven as Katie began working on the next round, her fingers clumsy with disuse. The spice jars felt foreign in her hands. She misjudged the cinnamon, and too much tumbled into the bowl in a soft brown heap.

"*Ach*," she muttered, scraping at the mound with the edge of the spoon, frustration rising hot in her throat.

Emma reached gently for the bowl. "It's alright, let's just start fresh."

"I'm not a child," Katie snapped… sharper than she meant to. The words cut the air between them like a blade.

Emma's expression stilled, then softened, her voice calm. "I didn't say you were."

A pause passed between them, thick and uncomfortable.

Katie looked down at her flour-dusted hands. Her breath caught as shame crept in, quiet but sure.

"I know you didn't," her voice lower now. "I just… I feel like one lately. Can't think straight, can't bake a pie without making a mess." Her eyes didn't lift, but her tone held something raw and real. "I keep saying things I don't mean. Especially to you and Daniel."

Emma didn't respond right away. She just reached for a clean bowl and placed it on the counter between them.

"Then we'll start again … just like the pies."

Katie looked at her then, and the sting of her outburst gave way to something softer. Gratitude. Love. The faintest thread of who she used to be weaving its way back in.

"I missed this," she admitted quietly. "Not the baking, exactly… but being here. With you."

Emma's eyes shimmered for just a second before she turned to the cupboard. "Then let's make it feel like home again."

Katie nodded, her hands already moving with more steadiness. The cinnamon was measured carefully this time.

The door chimed. Samuel walked in, wearing a grin, like always, and headed straight for the fried pies.

"Smells like fall in here." He winked at one of the girls. "Save me the best one, *jah*?"

Emma chuckled and handed him a wrapped fried pie. "Always do."

Samuel turned and spotted Katie. His smile widened. "*Goot* to see you back here, *schwester*."

Katie managed a nod.

Samuel moved to the table, leaning in beside Emma. "*Datt* might stop by. Something about the ledger from the last harvest."

Emma nodded. "I've been trying to sort through all that for him since your *mamm* passed."

Katie stiffened at the mention of her mother's name. Samuel's tone had been so casual. So… untouched.

He didn't look like someone who'd buried his mother three months ago.

"Samuel, do you even miss *Mamm*?"

The entire bakery fell silent.

Samuel blinked. "What?"

"You walk in here like everything's fine. You joke. You

laugh. You eat pies like you didn't just bury the best woman to ever walk this earth!"

Emma's mouth opened slightly, but she didn't speak.

Samuel stepped back, stunned. "Katie, we all don't process things the same way. I refuse to stop living… that isn't what *Mamm* would want for me or for you…"

Before he could say more, the door opened again, and Levi walked in, his cheeks red from the wind. "Morning, girls. Smells like Thanksgiving in here."

Katie's breath caught. The sight of her father, still managing to smile, still functioning, made something sharp twist deep in her chest.

Levi moved toward the counter, not yet noticing the tension.

Katie slammed her bowl down. "I can't do this."

She turned and fled into the back room, the door swinging behind her with a thud.

The stockroom was darker and cooler away from the ovens. Katie pressed her back to the wall and slid to the floor, her breath coming in shallow gasps. The dough still clung to her hands. She stared at it, hating the mess, hating herself.

On the other side of the door, she could hear murmurs.

Emma's voice. Samuel's. Then the low creak of the door opening slowly.

Emma knelt beside her.

Katie didn't look up.

"I know it's hard… I really do."

"*Nee*," Katie breathed. "You don't. You go on with your life. With your husband. With your children. You don't wake up every day thinking for just one second you might hear her voice, only to remember all over again that she's gone."

Emma's eyes shimmered. "I do know. I felt the same way when my *mamm* died. You're not alone."

Katie's throat tightened. "Then why does it feel like I am?"

Emma pulled a towel from the shelf and handed it to her. "Because heartache lies. It tells us we're the only ones hurting. But you're not. I see it in your *datt's* eyes. In Daniel's worry. In Mary's quietness."

Katie wiped her hands, then her face. "I messed everything up."

"You came today. That's not nothing."

Outside, Levi's low chuckle echoed faintly, and Katie flinched.

"I want to be okay again, Emma," she muttered. "But I don't

know how."

Emma gave her a long, steady look. "No one expects you to figure it out on your own."

***

The afternoon rush at the bakery had slowed. The bell above the door stood still for once, the sweet scents of fruit pies and cinnamon rolls lingering in the air.

Katie wiped her hands on a towel and strode to the front porch, hoping for a breath of stillness. Outside, the wind carried a light drizzle, not a downpour, just a ceaseless mist softening the edges of the gray early winter day.

She decided to grab the umbrella and walk to the end of the lane to gather the mail. Thumbing through the envelopes and advertisements from the local *Feed & Seed* and the *Budget Newspaper*, one plain white envelope stopped her in her tracks. Pittsburgh postmark. The same neat handwriting.

Her breath caught.

Emma appeared from the back, smoothing her apron. "Need me to pull another tray out?"

Katie shook her head faintly, eyes on the letter. "*Nee*… just taking a minute."

She eased herself onto the wooden bench near the front window, fingers trembling slightly as she opened the flap.

Emma tilted her head, curious. "You've gotten a few of those," she remarked softly. "From Pittsburgh?"

Katie hesitated, then, perhaps for the first time, didn't close herself off. Instead, she exhaled slowly. "It's from a woman... someone who knew *Mamm*. From the clinic."

Emma came closer, drying her hands. "Truly?"

Katie nodded. "She... she said *Mamm's* faith touched her while they were both patients." She unfolded the paper carefully, her heart both aching and expectant. Emma sat beside her without a word.

The letter was short this time:

*I wanted you to know I've been praying for you. Grieving with joy is something I learned late, too late for many things. But your mother taught me it's possible. I hope, in your own way, you find light in that, too. I've been painting again, and it's helped more than words can say. Sometimes doing something with your hands quiets the heart.*

*A Friend*

Katie read it twice. The words blurred a little, warmth pooling behind her eyes, not heavy like before, but something softer. Without thinking, she passed the letter to Emma.

Emma read quietly, her expression tender. When she looked up, her gaze shimmered. "*Ach*... that's beautiful."

"It is," Katie whispered. She pressed her palm to the paper. "It's strange, but... when her letters come, it feels like... *Mamm* is still reaching for me somehow."

Emma swallowed, voice low. "Maybe she is."

For a moment, neither spoke. The drizzle tapped against the windowpane, constant and light.

The doorbell jingled as a customer came in, but for just that moment, between letters, between friends, the healing continued its serene work.

The two young girls working that afternoon glanced up as the rain started to pelt the windowpane harder. Emma offered them a tight smile. "Go on home, girls. We're closing early today."

Without a question, they gathered their things, whispering as they slipped out the side door.

Emma didn't speak until the door closed behind them. Then,

with quiet precision, she filled the kettle and set it on the stove.

A few minutes later, Emma returned with two mugs of tea. She slid one across the table and took a seat opposite Katie.

For a long while, neither spoke.

"I remember when my *mamm* passed," Emma's voice yielded, heavy with memory. "You sat with me after the funeral. Didn't say much. Just sat. And when I started to cry, you handed me a cup of tea and a cinnamon roll and said, 'The world shouldn't be allowed to keep spinning when someone you love is gone.'"

Katie's gaze stayed fixed on her tea.

"I felt that. Still do sometimes. But you were there. Every day."

Katie's chin quivered, and Emma added, "I'm sorry I haven't been that for you."

Emma reached across the table and laid her hand lightly on Katie's. "I hate seeing you like this and not knowing how to help."

Katie's shoulders slumped. "I'm not sleeping. I feel sick most days. And I'm so tired. Not the kind that sleep fixes. The kind that buries you."

Emma's throat tightened. "Have you spoken to Daniel?"

Katie gave a bitter little laugh. "He sleeps on the daybed in the kitchen half the time. I don't blame him. I haven't been a *fraa* to him in months."

Emma nodded slowly. "Marriage takes hits in grief. But it doesn't have to stay broken."

"I don't even know who I am anymore," Katie moaned. "If it wasn't for Betty, the *kinner* would be living off bread and milk. I'm failing them all."

Emma leaned in. "You're not failing. You're hurting. There's a difference."

Katie's eyes welled up again.

Emma squeezed her hand. "Let's start small. Let's find a midwife or a counselor to talk to, someone who understands our ways and pain."

Katie didn't answer right away. But she nodded slowly.

Emma gave a weak smile. "*Jah*?"

***

The waiting room buzzed with muffled chatter, the occasional cry of a baby, and the hum of toys clinking together beneath the play table. Katie sat stiffly in a corner chair, her hands nestled against her skirt, her eyes fixed on the floor. Children's feet padded past her, some in worn boots, some in bright pink sneakers. Amish and *Englisch*. The worlds collided here in a strange, uneasy truce.

Her name echoed through the room, distant and too loud all at once.

"Katie Miller?"

She rose slowly, each step through the narrow hallway like walking through a dream, or a fog she couldn't quite lift. The walls were bright with cheerful colors, meant to calm, she guessed. But all Katie saw were the sterile tiles and the long stretch ahead.

The nurse, a young *Englisch* girl with a braid wound tight against her scalp, offered a gentle smile. "We'll be right with you. You can hop up on the table, and the midwife will be in shortly."

Katie nodded silently and obeyed. The paper crackled beneath her as she sat. The sharp scent of disinfectant clung to the air… sterile, cold, and uninviting. She rubbed her arms through the sleeves of her wool coat, chasing warmth that wouldn't come. Everything in the room was too bright, too white, as if it had never known sorrow, and standing in the middle of it, she barely recognized the shape of her own life anymore.

Emma had gently pressed her more than once to make the appointment. Daniel, lately, didn't press at all. He'd grown silent. Resigned.

She hated that she'd let things get this far.

She looked down at her hands. Pale. Fidgeting. Her mother's hands had never looked like this. Her mother's hands had been busy, strong, always kneading dough or cutting patterns or brushing her *kinner's* cheeks. Her hands hadn't been productive in months.

What would they say in here? That she was tired? That she cried too much? That it was normal to snap at her *kinner* for spilling juice or not folding towels right? That some mornings she couldn't even make herself get dressed?

Would they think she was a bad mother? The thought stung.

What if this midwife thought grief had lasted too long, that something darker had settled in? Would they suggest something worldly? Something her community wouldn't understand? Would they say the word "*depression*" out loud?

She shivered again and folded her arms tighter.

Maybe the midwife would just tell her what she already

knew. She wasn't herself and hadn't been in a long time.

Maybe… just maybe she needed help beyond what Daniel or Emma or even Betty could give. And that terrified her.

But still… she'd come. That counted for something.

Right?

A loud knock interrupted her spiral of thoughts.

Katie sat up straighter.

The door opened with a click, and in stepped a woman in a plain gray dress and *kapp*, her kind eyes framed by soft lines of age and understanding.

"*Guder Mariye*, Katie." Her voice was kind. "I'm Maryann. I hear you've been walking through a long, hard season."

Katie blinked at her. Then nodded, once.

The woman crossed the room and pulled up a chair.

"Let's talk a bit, *jah*? I understand you've been feeling overwhelmed lately."

Katie nodded, her eyes welling up. "I can't seem to find joy in anything. I'm constantly tired, and I don't feel well most days."

Maryann took a seat beside her, settling with the ease of someone used to quiet spaces. She opened the folder on her lap and made a few notes, then glanced up with a warm, even expression.

"Your feelings are valid. You're not alone in this. Many women feel overwhelmed after childbirth, even without grief weighing them down. Add in the loss of someone as central as your mother…" She trailed off, allowing the silence to honor the weight of it. "It's no wonder your heart feels heavy."

Katie said nothing, her hands knotted in on her lap.

Maryann continued, her tone calm but never distant. "We often look to natural remedies first: calming teas like lemon balm or chamomile, nourishing broths, daily walks, rest when you can get it." She offered a small smile. "Though I know rest can feel like a stranger when your thoughts won't sit still."

Katie's lips twitched, almost a smile. Almost.

"And while those things help the body," Maryann said more softly, "the soul needs tending too."

That made Katie flinch… barely, but Maryann noticed.

She didn't push. Instead, she pulled a small cloth pouch from a drawer and placed it into Katie's hands. The faint scent of lavender and dried mint rose up like a memory.

"My *grossmommi* used to say healing comes in layers. First the body, then the mind… and the spirit somewhere in between. When one is neglected, the others limp along."

Katie ran her thumb over the stitching on the pouch. "I've tried praying, but I don't hear anything. Nothing comes."

Maryann nodded slowly. "Sometimes the silence is the prayer."

Katie looked up, confused.

"There were days… after I had my stillborn daughter… when I couldn't pray either. I'd sit with my Bible closed on my lap and just weep. Not a word spoken. And still, He met me there."

Katie's eyes shimmered, but she blinked the tears away.

"I think sometimes we think we have to show up put together. Say the right words. Feel the right things. But *Gott* doesn't ask for perfection, Katie. Just presence. Just willingness."

A long pause passed between them.

"I don't know if I can do that."

"Start small. Sit outside with your tea. Say one sentence. Write it in a journal if speaking feels too hard. Or just breathe… and know He hears even that."

Katie stared down at the cloth pouch in her hands like it might anchor her.

Maryann rose, gathering her folder. "I won't pretend it's easy. But I do know that healing begins when we stop hiding from the One who sees us best. And He's not angry. He's waiting."

Katie swallowed hard. "*Dankie*."

Maryann smiled and reached and laid her hand on Katie's shoulder, just like a mother might. "You're not broken. Just bruised. And bruises heal best with kindness… especially toward yourself."

She crossed to the door, pausing once more before she stepped out. "Let yourself be cared for. By others. By Him. And by you."

After a thoughtful pause, Maryann added, "I'd like to run some blood tests to check for any underlying issues, such as anemia or thyroid imbalances, which can contribute to your symptoms."

Katie agreed, and a nurse soon came in to draw her blood. As she waited for the results, Katie reflected on the midwife's words, feeling a glimmer of hope that there might be an underlying issue that was contributing to her state of mind.

Thirty minutes later, Maryann knocked softly before stepping back into the room. She held a small clipboard in her hand and wore a gentle, sound expression.

"Katie," she began, easing onto the stool beside her, "the bloodwork shows you're with child again."

Katie blinked at her, stunned. "*Nee*," shaking her head before the word even settled in the air. "That… that can't be." Her hands trembled in her lap. "Danny is only eight months. How—"

Maryann waited, saying nothing, just allowing the silence to rest between them.

"I can't do this again," Katie choked. "I'm barely managing with the three I have. I don't sleep, I can't even keep my thoughts straight, and now… now this?" Her voice cracked. "What kind of mother would I be to another *boppli* when I can't even take care of the ones I have?"

Maryann's expression softened with understanding. "I know this feels heavy, like another stone on an already full load. But you must remember, we don't walk these burdens alone… not in faith, and not in our community."

Katie let out a breath that quivered, looking down at her hands. "Everyone expects me to be fine. But I'm not fine. I'm tired. Angry. And now I'm going to have another child I didn't even ask for." Her shoulders shook. "How am I supposed to feel joy when I can barely breathe?"

Maryann's voice was calm but firm. "You don't have to feel joy today. But in time, joy will come again. *Gott* gives us what we need, sometimes even before we know how to use it."

She leaned forward. "You're not expected to carry this alone. It's not our way. Just like your *mamm* would've done for another, they'll do for you. You need to let them."

Katie's lips pressed together as tears spilled down her cheeks.

"This new *boppli,*" Maryann continued quietly, "isn't here to make your life harder. Maybe *Gott* sent it to help bring you back. To give you a new reason to reach for the light again."

Katie let her head fall forward, a sob catching in her throat. "I don't know if I'm strong enough."

"You don't need to be strong alone." Maryann's voice was like the hush of a hymn. "You just need to take one step, then another. And let the rest of us take the steps you cannot until you can again."

Katie nodded slowly, her body trembling with exhaustion and something that felt dangerously close to surrender. Not the giving-up kind, but the giving-in kind, like allowing a lifeboat to carry her when she'd fought the water too long.

# CHAPTER 8

The kitchen of the Yoder farmhouse smelled like memories. Katie stepped through the back door with Danny bundled against her shoulder, the comfort of the kitchen enveloping her like a well-worn quilt. Roast turkey, slow-cooked green beans, and cinnamon-sweet squash perfumed the air. Betty stood at the stove stirring gravy while Emma arranged her famous pecan and shoofly pies on the sideboard.

Katie's eyes drifted to the long table stretched across the room, where the good dishes had been set out and the chairs pushed close to make room for everyone. It should've felt comforting, coming home for Thanksgiving, but all she could feel was the hollow ache where her mother should've been.

Emma met her at the door, brushing a strand of hair from her flour-smudged face. "We're glad you're here."

Katie forced a smile. "We brought the dinner rolls. They didn't rise quite right."

"Does anyone notice after they're covered in butter?" Emma grinned, reaching for the basket. "Come. Sit."

Levi emerged from the front room, his gait slower than usual, his hands freshly scrubbed. His eyes flicked to the empty chair at the head of the table. The room stilled.

"I thought we'd leave your mother's place open… just to remember."

No one disagreed. Instead, Betty took a seat on the other side of Levi as they all bowed their heads.

Katie's throat tightened as she looked at the empty chair beside her father. The blue cushion still bore the imprint of her mother's form even though it hadn't been sat in for months.

Dinner passed in a quiet rhythm. Samuel teased Emma for overcooking the stuffing, and she swatted at him with a cloth napkin. Daniel balanced Danny on his knee while sneaking bites of stuffing. The children giggled over cranberry jelly and passed pumpkin pie as if their grandmother's absence wasn't a gaping hole at the table. But for once, the sound of their laughter didn't sting. It softened something inside everyone.

Later, after the table had been cleared and the dishes washed with the familiar hum of many hands working in tandem, Emma nudged Katie's elbow.

"Come with me for a minute."

Curious, Katie followed her through the hallway, past the coat pegs and the pantry door, until they strode into the sewing room. A shaft of afternoon sunlight streamed in through the window, catching the dust motes as they danced through the air.

There, stretched tight in the wooden frame near the window, was the quilt. Emma pulled the white sheet away, letting the blues and yellows leap off the still quilt frame. The dahlia pattern still held the shape of her mother's vision, radiating petals, stitched in practiced rows.

Katie approached it slowly, her fingers brushing over the fabric like it might speak. One of the needles still rested where her mother had last left it, thread dangling like a breath caught mid-sentence.

Emma touched the edge gently. "I thought maybe we could finish it. Together."

Katie turned to her, startled.

Emma continued, her voice softer now. "We used to stitch together, remember? Sometimes just for the company. Maybe it would be healing for both of us."

They stood there for a while, shoulder to shoulder, the impact of shared grief settling between them, not heavy like it once was, but softer now, quilted and worn, warmed by memory.

Katie nodded. “Maybe.”

***

Katie stood at the kitchen table putting away the leftovers she’d brought home from Thanksgiving dinner. The evening had drawn long, the children tucked in, their bellies full and cheeks still rosy from playing with cousins and sneaking extra pie. Daniel sat near the hearth, reading *The Budget*, his face peaceful for the first time in weeks, and Betty had already gone to bed.

Katie turned toward the counter where she had set the week’s mail earlier. A modest stack lay where she had left it: seed catalogs, the oil bill, and one envelope with handwriting she recognized instantly.

Her fingers trembled slightly as she lifted the letter. That same soft, slanted script. Postmarked from Pittsburgh, just like the last ones, but this time a return address was added.

Katie stepped slowly into the front room, pulled the rocking chair close to the lamp, and settled in. She opened the envelope and unfolded the letter with slow reverence.

*Dear Katie,*

*I hope it's not too bold of me to write again, but I wanted to share something with you. I, too, lost my mother when my children were still little. I was only twenty-five, with a newborn on my hip and another child barely able to walk.*

*The ache of that sorrow... it settled into me like cold in my bones. I remember feeling angry all the time, at my husband, at the children, at myself. I thought maybe I was broken. I was afraid I'd never be the same again, that I'd never find the old me.*

Katie paused, her throat tightening as she read. She glanced toward Daniel, who was nodding off in his chair, a weak whimper escaping her lips.

*I wish I could say exactly how long it took for the ache to ease. But one day, I was brushing my daughter's hair and realized I was humming the same lullaby my mother used to sing. And in that moment, I knew I hadn't lost her completely. She was with me still, in the way I folded laundry, in the recipes I cooked, in the way I comforted my children.*

*I just wanted to encourage you that you don't have to be strong every day. But you do have to keep stepping forward, even if it's just one step at a time. I pray for you every morning that God will send just enough strength to make the next step. I promise you they will get easier over time.*

*Yours in grace,*

*A Friend Who Understands*

Katie's eyes were swimming with tears. There were no loud revelations, no lightning-strike changes, just that quiet voice again, so much like her mother whispering from a place beyond pain. A reminder that others had walked this path before her and the healing was slow, but not impossible.

She closed her eyes and whispered into the quietness of the farmhouse, "*Dankie*, Lord… for sending her. For knowing just what I needed to hear."

***

A week later, a new chill had crept into the early December air, and Katie sat at the kitchen table wrapped in a knitted sweater, her mug of mint tea long gone cold beside her.

She walked to the drawer near the back door, fingertips brushing across a stack of simple stationery. The top page bore a picture of a coffee cup and a pair of cinnamon rolls, steam curling upward into a pretty script that read: *"Be still, and know that I am God."*

Katie stared at the verse a long moment, her thumb tracing its edges as if it alone might lend her the strength to begin.

She sat back at the table, uncapped her pen, and slowly began to write.

*Dear Friend,*

*I wasn't sure I'd write back, but your letter... it felt like a breath of fresh air I didn't think I needed. Thank you for your honesty. For your prayers. For sharing your own story so freely with a stranger who doesn't even know your name. You may not believe this, but I think God sent you to me.*

*I read your letter twice the day I opened it, and again this morning before sunrise. And still, it makes me cry. But not the kind of cry that comes from lost hope, more like the kind that lets you breathe after holding it in too long.*

She paused, her eyes clouding before she carefully continued.

*There's something I haven't told anyone yet, not even my husband. I just found out I'm with child again. Our Danny is only eight months old, and this news doesn't bring me the joy I think it should. It feels wrong to let myself feel any happiness when my mother isn't here to enjoy it.*

*Some mornings I wake up and wonder if I'll ever be the woman my mamm was. She was strong and sure, the kind of woman who kept a household running with nothing but her quiet sureness. She had a peace about her that made even hard things feel bearable. I don't have that. Not even close.*

Her handwriting slowed.

*I snap too easily at my girls. I wear my husband's patience thin. And when I look at the days ahead, instead of hope, I just feel tired. My mother would've known what to do, how to comfort Daniel, how to raise our kinner with gentleness. She was a good wife to my father. And here I am, wondering if I even deserve the life I've been given.*

*Still, your words remind me I'm not as alone as I thought. That maybe, somewhere inside, the woman I want to be still exists. Maybe she's just buried for now.*

*Please don't feel like you need to write again. But I needed to say thank you. For your kindness. For reminding me that others have felt this and have come out the other side.*

*Your letter was like a whisper from heaven. One that reminded me that maybe my mother is still with me, just in a different way.*

*With a humbled heart,*

*Katie Miller*

Katie folded the letter carefully, slid it into an envelope, and held it a moment before rising from the table. She walked it to the mailbox at the end of the lane, her shoes crunching against the frostbitten ground, her breath like smoke in the morning air.

As she slipped the envelope into the box and raised the flag, a flicker of warmth tangled in her heart. No, she didn't feel strong yet. Not even close. But maybe, just maybe, the stranger helped her take one small step toward healing.

***

The wind cut across the pasture as Daniel tugged the lead rope, guiding the young Standardbred gelding toward the circle. The horse tossed its head, nostrils flaring with impatience. Samuel stood in the center of the training pen, his arms crossed, and his collar pulled up against the cold.

"Still wants to run, doesn't he?" Samuel called out, watching the horse sidestep with restless energy.

Daniel grunted, adjusting his grip. "That's all they've ever known. Speed. Winning. Racing hard and being handled rough."

"Kind of like people," Samuel motioned for Daniel to circle the gelding again. "You train 'em with a whip, they think that's the only way to go. Takes time to teach 'em slow and steady is better."

Daniel raised a brow. "You talkin' about the horse or me?"

Samuel chuckled and shrugged. "Both maybe."

Daniel looked away as he sent the gelding into a lope around the ring. Dust and dried grass kicked up under its hooves, echoing the agitation inside him. He hadn't slept much the past few weeks, not since Katie and his talk that ended with him on the daybed and her wrapped in resistance.

Samuel finally spoke. "How's it going with Katie?"

Daniel led the horse to the fence. "She's trying. Might not look like it, but just coming to Thanksgiving dinner, saying she'd work on that quilt with Emma… that was something. Better than nothing."

Daniel sighed. "She's still not herself. She won't talk to me unless it's about the *kinner*. It's like she's only halfway here, holding something back."

"And yet," Samuel tossed a rope over the fence, "she's still showin' up, even if it's messy."

Daniel slid the harness from the gelding's back, hanging it over the stall gate with a practiced motion. The horse let out a slow breath, ears twitching as he ran to the other side of the corral.

"He's not nearly as wild as when he first came in."

"*Jah*," Daniel brushed dust from his sleeves. "He's got some fight in him still, but he wants to learn."

They stood in silence a moment, the kind that sat easy between men who'd worked side by side most days.

Daniel didn't answer right away. He picked up the bucket, filled it from the pump, and set it down near the feed bins before he spoke.

"Some days, I see a glimmer of her again. Other days… nothing." He wiped his hands on a rag. "But I've stopped waiting for the old Katie to come back. I think… maybe that's not the point."

Samuel raised a brow.

Daniel leaned against the stall, his voice low and steady. "I think she's becoming someone new. And I'm trying to learn how to be a husband to the new Katie."

Samuel gave a slow nod. "That takes courage."

"I've got determination. And I've got *Gott*. So I figure that's enough to carry us for now."

Another beat passed.

"You remember when I shut down after we lost the baby? Wouldn't talk to anyone, not even you?"

Daniel nodded.

"You walked with me through that season. Never pushed, never left. You were just present." Samuel turned, leaning against the beam beside him. "Then don't lose hope. Katie's still in there. Might take longer than you'd like, but she'll find her way. Especially with you steady beside her."

They stood for a few minutes in a comfortable silence, both lost in their own thoughts, before Daniel finally added, "I used to watch the window every morning, wondering if it would be the day she'd come back to herself. Now I just ask the Lord to help me see the good that's still there."

"That's something," Samuel replied, standing and brushing off his hands.

Daniel shrugged. "I figure love's not about fixing her. It's about being the one thing that doesn't walk away when everything else falls apart."

They stood looking out over the pasture. Samuel gave Daniel a look that said more than words ever could. Pride. Respect. Brotherhood.

Daniel brushed his hat off on his leg, the brim catching a glint of late light. He didn't rush, just stood there a beat longer, eyes on the horizon beyond the pasture.

"I think I'll take the girls fishing this Sunday. Let her have the *haus* to herself. Maybe the Lord can reach her better without me hovering."

Samuel nodded, quiet approval in his eyes.

Daniel shifted the brim of his hat between his hands. "Hardest part of being a *mun*," he muttered, "is learning I can't fix everything."

He set the hat on his head and started for the barn door.

"Sometimes," he added over his shoulder, "the best thing I can do for Katie is step back… and stay out of *Gott's* way."

***

Betty's knife moved easily through the carrots, the sharp snap of each slice keeping time with the rustle of feet behind her. She didn't turn as Mary guided Ella through drying the last supper plate. The little girl's arms barely reached the towel draped over the counter, and Betty could see the tip of her pink tongue poking out with effort.

She turned, lightly wiping her hands on her apron. "Mary, why don't you take Ella and go check on the *boppli* for your *mamm*?"

Mary hesitated, glancing toward her mother at the stove, then nodded. Ella trailed behind her like a duckling.

Betty waited until she heard their bare feet slap against the polished steps before speaking. "You're quiet."

Katie stirred the pot of noodles. "Got lots on my mind, I reckon."

Betty gave a knowing smile. "Something weighing heavy… I can tell, but it's best you work through it on your own, I suppose, *jah*?"

Katie didn't respond.

"I've been thinking," Betty took a seat at the table and motioned Katie to do the same. "It's time for me to head back home."

Katie stopped stirring. "You're leaving?"

"Soon, *jah*. Not tonight or tomorrow, but after the new year. You need to start walking this life on your own two feet again."

Katie turned, eyes wide and worried. "But… what if I'm not ready? What if I fall back into that dark place?"

Betty moved closer, resting a firm hand on her shoulder. "Then you'll get back up. With *Gott's* help, and with Daniel, and your family. You've come further than you know."

Katie looked away, voice low. "I don't feel like I've come far at all."

"You have," Betty said, steady. "You just ain't seen it yet. But I have. I see how you hold Danny closer now. I see how you look at your girls like you're tryin' to remember what joy feels like. And even this, cooking supper. You weren't doing that three months ago."

Katie's hands gripped the wooden spoon. "It still hurts so much, and I don't want to do Christmas without her."

Betty's own throat tightened. "None of us do. That's why I'll stay through the holidays. But come January, you'll have to start waking up with a plan for the day on your own again."

Katie nodded slowly, tears brimming.

At that moment, the girls' voices rang out as they came downstairs, Ella giggling as she plugged her tiny nose. "Ew! He stinks!"

Mary's small but determined steps followed quickly behind, her arms wrapped around Danny's middle as she carried him carefully down the stairs.

"He made a big mess," she announced, half-exasperated, half-proud of her ability to handle it.

Katie turned just in time to see Mary lay the baby gently on the daybed in the corner. She retrieved the changing cloth from the side table, wiped his fussing face with a soft hum, and reached for a fresh diaper like she'd done it a hundred times before.

The ease of it, the practiced way her five-year-old handled what should've been a mother's job, hit Katie hard.

Betty moved beside her and watched discreetly. "You see that?"

Katie swallowed hard, unable to take her eyes off her daughter.

"She's been carrying more than just her little brother these past months." Betty's voice stayed low and kind, but the edge in it couldn't be ignored. "That's your job now. It's time you took it back."

Katie nodded slowly, her throat thick.

"She needs to go back to being a kind, silly big *schwester*, not a second mother. She needs space to play. To be five. You need to take that weight off her shoulders."

"I didn't mean to put it there," Katie sighed.

"I know, but it happened. And it's not too late to fix it."

Mary finished diapering her *bruder* and kissed his chubby cheek before lifting him into her arms. She turned to find them watching her and smiled shyly.

Katie wiped her hands on her apron and crossed the room. "I'll take him, *dankie*"

Mary hesitated only a second, then passed Danny to her. "He's happier now."

Katie held her son close, her arms suddenly aching with the weight she hadn't carried enough. She pressed her face into his neck and inhaled deeply, the scent of baby powder breaking something open inside her.

Betty stood back and smiled. "That's a good start."

Katie didn't respond. She was too focused on the warm body in her arms, and the faint sound of her own heart remembering how to feel.

# CHAPTER 9

The air was brisk as Betty made her way across the yard that stretched between Katie's and Levi's. She balanced a warm apple pie in one hand and held her scarf tight to her chin with the other. The steps creaked under her shoes, and she knocked once before stepping inside, calling tenderly, "Levi?"

"In here," came the low reply.

She found him at the kitchen table, a newspaper open in front of him, though he didn't seem to be reading. Just staring at it, hands folded around a half-full mug of cold coffee.

"I brought pie. It's still warm."

A faint smile lifted one corner of his mouth. "Didn't realize how much I missed apple pie until just now."

Without waiting, Betty moved toward the stove and filled the kettle. "Let's make us some fresh coffee. You can't have pie with cold coffee. That would be a waste."

Levi gave a throaty chuckle, rubbing the back of his neck as if embarrassed by the comfort her presence brought. "I've never been good at offering company. Ruth… she did all that."

"I know," she set out two mugs and sliced the pie. "And I'm not looking for company. Just offering a friend to share a few peaceful minutes with."

They sat, the silence between them familiar but not uncomfortable. Outside, the wind rattled the loose pane in the kitchen window. Levi took a bite and nodded appreciatively.

"This is *goot.* Really *goot*."

A calm settled again before Levi's voice cut through, slower this time. "How's Katie this morning?"

"Coming along," Betty poured coffee into both mugs. "Not out of the woods yet, but I see more light in her eyes than I did a few weeks ago."

He sighed and looked toward the wall as if he could see his daughter through it. "I haven't known how to help her. Sometimes, I think just being around me makes it worse. I remind her too much of Ruth."

"She's getting there," and with a sly smile, she added, "now that she doesn't need me every hour, maybe it's you I need to keep an eye on."

He looked at her then, surprised. "Me?"

"You've been keeping yourself too quiet, Levi Yoder. You've spent so much time trying not to upset anyone else that you forgot to grieve for yourself."

His eyes dropped to the rim of his mug, and he cleared his throat. "Not sure how to do that out loud."

"You don't have to, but don't do it alone."

The words settled between them, light and meaningful. He nodded once. "I'm glad you're here."

"I won't be for long. I told Katie I'd stay through Christmas. But come the new year… it'll be time for me to go home."

Levi's brow creased. "We'll miss you."

"I'll miss all of you. But the whole point of helping someone stand is so they can walk on their own again at some point."

He lifted his mug in an unofficial toast. "To standing again."

She raised hers to meet his. "And not alone."

***

Levi stood at the kitchen window long after Betty had gone. Her plate and coffee mug sat clean in the drying rack beside the sink, and the scent of cinnamon and apples still lingered in the air.

The empty chair beside him tugged at something deep within him. It had sat with Ruth perched in it, going over her day and adding peace and joy to his. He reached out and ran his hand across the worn wood of the back of her chair.

Sorrow was a strange thing. It snuck up on you when the house was empty, when the clatter of dishes was gone and the last echoes of laughter faded. When the rooms felt just a shade too big, it pressed on your chest at night, made you turn over in bed, only to find cool sheets where a warm shoulder used to be.

He walked to the coat hooks near the back door, pulled down Ruth's old shawl, the deep blue one she wore in fall, and pressed it to his face. The smell was faint now. Just a whisper of lavender. He folded it carefully and returned it to the peg.

Outside, the garden was brown and brittle, the mums she had loved now dried and bowed low under the weight of last night's frost. The first real snow hadn't come yet, but it was close. The earth was preparing to rest.

Just like Ruth had.

Betty's words echoed in his mind.

You forgot to grieve for yourself.

Had he? Or had he just learned to carry it so quietly that even he stopped hearing it?

He'd tried to stay strong for the *kinner*, for Katie. But maybe he'd leaned so far into himself he left no space for mourning.

And now… now there was Betty Troyer.

He hadn't expected her. Not the way she could sit in silence without making it awkward, or how she gave a quiet nudge when he needed it most. She didn't hover or ask too much. Just saw him, clear and steady. And somehow, that was enough to steady something in him too.

He wasn't ready for anything more. It was too soon. Ruth's memory still felt like something sacred, something that couldn't be set aside for something new.

But maybe, just maybe, it was all right to let someone sit across the table now and then.

Levi stepped outside, letting the cold slap his cheeks as he walked toward the shed. There was always work to be done. But maybe tonight, he'd stop by Katie and Daniel's place. Maybe bring some candy for the girls. And maybe just sit at the kitchen table again, with people who were still here.

***

Emma wiped the counter with rhythmic strokes, the scent of yeast lingering in the air. The bakery was still, the morning rush long past. She paused as she glanced out the front window toward the road.

Across the street, Betty was stepping down Levi's front porch, her hands wrapped around an empty pie plate. Emma's brows lifted, and she tilted her head to follow the older woman's solid steps back toward the Miller home.

"*Hmm*," she murmured softly.

The front door creaked open behind her, and Samuel walked inside, brushing off his hat and stomping light bits of straw from his boots.

"Samuel, come here a minute." She waved him over with the cloth still in her hand, her eyes still trained on the window as she pointed across the street. "Look."

He peered over her shoulder, his body warm behind hers. "Betty's been visiting *Datt.*"

Emma nodded slowly. "That's the second time this week."

Samuel chuckled, wrapping his arms gently around her, his hands instinctively settling over the curve of her belly. "You sound more like the ladies who come in here for gossip and fritters."

She elbowed him lightly but tipped into his embrace. "I'm just… surprised is all."

He kissed the top of her head. "She's a widow. He's a widower. Stranger things have happened."

Emma sighed. "It's not that. I'm glad he has someone to talk to. It's just that everything feels so heavy lately. Betty brings a lightness to this family in a special way, *jah*?"

He shifted so she could face him and changed the subject while his hand stayed right where it had landed.

"You're going to have to tell them soon, you know?"

Emma's hand rested over his. "I know."

"Can't hide this much longer." He gave her an easy grin. "Not that you ever could. You grow rounder with each *boppli* sooner than the last."

A smile tugged at the corner of her mouth. "I wanted to wait. Katie's been so fragile. I didn't want to press joy into a space still soaked in misery."

"I'd think she'd be happy for you."

Emma looked down, brushing the cloth over the already clean countertop. "I hope so. I've been walking on eggshells around her, waiting for the right time. But maybe the right time won't ever come. I just need to step forward and trust."

Samuel nodded. "You've always had a way of reading people, and you'll know when the time is right."

"I plan to tell her this week. Maybe when we're elbow-deep in pie dough." She gave a subtle laugh. "That's when we do our best talking."

"You're doing a *goot* job being her friend."

They stood there a moment longer, watching the wind tug at the bare branches outside. Betty had disappeared around the back of the Miller house, and Levi's screen door gently bounced shut in her wake.

Maybe healing had its own subtle rhythm, Emma thought. One minute, one pie, one friend at a time.

***

The knock on the door was soft, two quick taps that made her pause as Katie folded one of Danny's blankets over the back of the rocker. For a second, she thought about ignoring it. But when she peeked out the window and saw her father standing on the porch, his hands tucked in his coat pockets and shoulders slightly hunched, something inside her stirred.

"*Datt*?"

"Afternoon, Katie." Levi stepped inside. "Didn't mean to interrupt. Thought I'd check in, see how you're getting on."

She nodded and motioned for him to come in. "We're fine. Daniel's out at the barn. Betty's resting. The *kinner* are quiet for once."

Levi chuckled lightly and followed her into the front room, where they settled into the rockers near the window. Katie sat opposite him, her fingers fussing with the corner of the blanket over her lap. They sat for a moment, the clock ticking between them like a distraction.

"I sense you and Daniel are having a rough patch?"

Katie's lips tightened, but she nodded. "It's been hard. On both of us."

Levi leaned forward, resting his arms on his knees. "It happens. More than folks talk about."

She looked up, surprised to see the weariness in her father's eyes. He wasn't a man of many words. Never had been. But now, something in his expression had eased… quiet, unspoken, almost tender.

"Your mother and I had our own struggles early on, before you or Samuel came along. We lost three babies, one after the other. Hardest time of our lives."

Katie's eyes widened. She'd heard whispered mentions of a loss but never knew it had happened more than once.

Levi rubbed a hand over his jaw. "We didn't talk about it much. No one really does. But loss, especially when it keeps returning, it changes things. Makes it easy to turn away from each other instead of toward."

Katie swallowed hard. "How did you and *Mamm* get through it?"

"We stopped trying to fix it all ourselves." He paused for a few moments before he continued. "I listened more. She forgave quicker. We learned that the strongest marriages don't happen because they never face hardship, but because they don't give up when they do."

Katie blinked against the tears threatening to fall. "I've been angry," she admitted. "At her… she left too soon. I wasn't ready."

"I know, and she knew it too."

Katie's gaze snapped to his face.

"The night before she passed," his voice lower now, "she asked me to remind you of something."

Katie closed her eyes, a tear slipping free down her cheek.

"She told me she saw in you the kind of faith that doesn't come from ease, but from choosing to stand again after falling hard. That you'd forget that for a while, and it was alright. But you'd find your way back."

Her hands curled on her lap. "She said that?"

Levi nodded. "She did. She knew you. Better than any of us."

A long pause stretched between them, thick with emotion. The fire popped in the hearth. The light through the window fell over Levi's face, softening the edges of his normally stoic features.

"I've missed her every day," Katie muttered.

"So have I," Levi replied, his voice thick. "But a part of her is still here. Because she's a part of you."

"I haven't been easy to live with. Daniel's been patient, but… I've pushed him away."

Levi stood, crossing to her. He laid a large, weathered hand on her shoulder. "Then start small. Say one kind word. Share one meal together. Let him hold your hand again. The rest will come."

She nodded slowly, her heart aching with both the weight and the comfort of his words.

As he turned to leave, he paused at the door.

"I thought I was coming to check on you." Levi smiled. "Turns out your *mamm* sent me to deliver a message instead."

Katie gave a tearful laugh. "She always did know what I needed before I did."

As the door clicked shut behind him, Katie sat in the stillness, clutching the tenderness of her mother's love spoken through her father's voice. Another whisper from heaven.

***

Katie wasn't sure how long she sat in the quiet, the fire crackling low behind her and the echo of her father's words lingering in the air. Her mind traced the simple truths he'd shared, how pain had once strained his own marriage, how *Mamm* had seen through the storm that was sure to come after her passing.

For months, she'd been looking for healing in all the wrong places, avoiding the pain, burying the ache, blaming others for moving forward while she stayed stuck in sorrow.

She stood slowly, the rocker creaking beneath her as she stepped toward the old hutch by the window. Her fingers reached for the small box tucked on the top shelf, the one where she kept her most precious things.

The letter her mother had penned just weeks before she passed was folded neatly and sealed with care.

She had carried it for weeks in her apron pocket, moved it from nightstand to dresser, and finally tucked it away in the box. She had read the first line more than once, only to break down in sobs that left her breathless.

She eased the envelope open and pulled out the crisp, lined paper. Her mother's familiar handwriting flowed across the page in blue ink, steady and sure.

*My dearest Katie,*

*If you're reading this, I've gone on to be with the Lord. Don't let that first sentence scare you. I'm not gone, not really. Just walking ahead of you for a while…*

Katie swallowed hard, but the tears didn't come. Not this time.

*You're stronger than you believe. You always have been. You carry the hearts of those you love so deeply, it's why you feel pain like this. But that same heart is what will lead you back to joy someday. Let it.*

The lines blurred slightly, but she blinked the tears back, determined now to read every word.

*Love Daniel. Even when it's hard. Love those sweet kinner. Let them see you laugh again. That laughter will come. Not today. Maybe not tomorrow. But it will.*

Katie held the letter as if it might tear, as she stood in the dim afternoon light spilling through the pulled-back blue curtain. Her fingers trembled. The stillness around her shifted, quiet, almost sacred. As if her mother had just stepped out of the room. As if hope had been waiting there all along, tucked into the shadows.

# CHAPTER 10

Snow blew against the windows, a constant hush that made everything inside feel stiller than usual. Betty stood in the front room, her bags neatly packed and set beside the front door.

Katie rubbed her hands down the sides of her apron, trying not to look as unsure as she felt. Betty's winter shawl was already tucked snug beneath her coat, her bonnet strings tied, as she slipped her feet into her boots. She looked every bit the sturdy, unshakable woman Katie had come to depend on.

She reached for her gloves but paused, turning toward Katie, her eyes full of something deeper than affection. "You'll be fine, and I'm just a short ride away if you need me. But I'm certain you won't."

Snow filtered down in thick, lazy sheets outside the window. The sleigh waited at the side of the porch, the mare's breath puffing in the crisp air as they stepped out on the porch. Levi stood nearby, bundled against the cold, hands in his coat pockets, giving them space.

Betty stepped beside her as she put on her gloves. "You're stronger than you think."

Katie's throat tightened. "Am I?"

"You are." Betty turned to face her and took both of Katie's hands in her gloved ones. "You're not who you were two months ago. Or even two weeks ago. You've faced the dark, and you're still standing. The Lord hasn't left you. And I'm not either. I'll be back in a few days to check on you. But this part? This part is yours now."

Footsteps thundered out the door, and Mary burst into Betty's arms. Ella trailed behind, clutching her baby doll and blinking back tears.

"Don't go!" Mary cried, wrapping her arms around Betty's middle. "We need you. Who's going to help me bake cookies?"

Ella tugged on Betty's skirts. "Who's gonna fix my mittens?"

Katie's heart twisted. The desperation in her children's voices, real, raw, cut deeper than anything they'd said to her in weeks.

Betty bent to their level and smoothed a hand over Mary's cheek. "Now listen here, sweet girls. Your *mamm* is strong. She's got everything you need and then some. And she knows how to fix mittens and bake cookies better than I do." Her gaze lifted and locked with Katie's.

Katie could hardly breathe.

"She needed my help for a little while, but she doesn't anymore. Not like before. It's time for your *mamm* to be your everything again."

The girls looked uncertain. Katie dropped to her knees beside them, reaching out to gather them close.

"I'm here," she whispered, pressing kisses to their heads. "I'm really here now."

Mary sniffed and turned into her. Ella slipped her fingers into Katie's hand.

"I'm sorry," Katie murmured as she stood. "That they… that I…"

"No apologies, child." Betty smoothed the arm of Katie's sweater, the gesture maternal and final. "They loved me because I stood in the gap. Now it's your turn to fill that spot again."

Katie gave a nod, tears thick in her eyes. Her gaze drifted to her father standing silently by the sleigh.

Betty moved down the steps, her silhouette sturdy against the gray morning sky. The girls moved to watching from the front window, their breath fogging the glass, small hands pressed to the pane.

Katie didn't move.

Not until the sleigh disappeared beyond the trees did she step back inside to shut it and rested the back of her head against it, muttering, "I can do this."

***

The next morning, steam curled from the teapot on the stove, and the faint scent of oatmeal filled the air. Katie sat stiffly in her chair, her hands wrapped around a mug that had long gone cold, trying to ward off the wave of depression that had once again settled in in the wee hours of the morning. She wasn't even sure what triggered it, but a black cloud had followed her to the kitchen.

Mary quietly scooped a ladle of oatmeal into Ella's bowl and added a drizzle of honey. The five-year-old's brow furrowed with concentration, trying not to spill, while Ella chattered to her rag doll in a whisper only the doll could hear.

Daniel sat across from Katie, elbows on the table, his eyes heavy from another night spent on the daybed. His shirt was wrinkled, and his beard was slightly uneven, signs of a man who was holding the pieces of a family together with his bare hands.

Katie pushed her spoon around in the bowl, barely tasting the bites she forced herself to swallow.

"I can get Danny dressed after breakfast," Mary offered quietly, glancing between her parents as she reached for a dishcloth to wipe Ella's sticky hands.

Katie's voice cut through the air like the sharp crack of a branch. "I'll do it."

Mary froze, her small hand resting on the edge of the table. "I just thought—"

"You think too much," Katie muttered, instantly regretting the words as they left her mouth.

Daniel's fork clattered against his plate. "Enough."

Katie looked up, startled by the firmness in his voice. He didn't shout, but the edge was there. The girls went still.

"She was only trying to help," Daniel added, not unkindly, but with a tiredness that made Katie flinch.

The silence that followed rang louder than any argument. Katie turned her gaze back to her bowl. Ella slowly picked up her spoon again, eyes down. Mary sat on her hands and stared at her own bowl.

Daniel stood and moved to refill his cup from the pot on the stove, but his movements were jerky and restless. The cloak of too many unsaid things filled the room like steam off boiling water.

"I'll take care of the horses. I'll be in the barn if you need me." The screen door creaked as he marched out, and then the familiar thud of his boots on the porch made Katie cringe as the door banged shut behind him.

Katie stared after him, her heart hollow.

Mary slid out of her chair without a word and began clearing the table.

Katie wanted to apologize, to gather her daughter into her arms and take back the sharp edge of her words. But her legs wouldn't move. Her voice sat buried somewhere deep, just out of reach, as if even the air between them had thickened.

She sat there, surrounded by the morning's wreckage, the scent of oatmeal, and the echo of her own unraveling again... the pressure to carry the load alone was too heavy.

***

That evening, Katie sat in the rocking chair by the window. Sleep eluded her yet again, so she came to sit by the fire. Her eyes were fixed on the corner of the room, where Daniel lay curled up under a patchwork quilt on the daybed.

He hadn't returned to their bed in weeks.

But tonight, her heart ached in ways she didn't have the words for, the space between them felt hollow.

Daniel stirred, rolling onto his back. He blinked, disoriented for a moment, before his eyes found her in the dark.

"You alright?" he whispered, his voice low and rough with sleep.

She nodded too quickly. "Couldn't sleep."

He sat up slowly. Studied her like he was trying to read what she wouldn't say. He looked so tired. Not just from the long days in the barn or the pressure of fatherhood, but something deeper. Something she knew she'd put there.

"I don't sleep well when you're not beside me."

His eyes widened slightly, surprised by her honesty. "I didn't think you wanted me there anymore."

Katie looked down at her hands. "I don't know what I want. I just know this… isn't working."

Daniel leaned forward, elbows on his knees. "No, it isn't."

Silence thickened again, pressing in around them.

Daniel stood and crossed the room slowly, but he didn't reach for her.

A tear slid down her cheek.

This time, he did reach for her. He crouched in front of her, his hands resting lightly on her knees. "I miss you, too."

She didn't answer, just stared at him with glassy eyes.

"I need you to come back to me," he breathed. "Not all at once. Not even tonight. But I need to know you're still in there somewhere. That I haven't lost you to someplace we'll never find again."

He stood and offered her his hand.

Katie hesitated, then slowly rose, placing her hand in his as he led her upstairs. The small act didn't fix anything. It didn't erase the weeks of reserve, the snapped words, or the ache that still wrapped itself around her ribs like barbed wire.

Without another word, he closed the distance between them and set the pillow on his side of the bed. Sitting down beside her, he let out a long sigh, the kind that sounded like months of tension loosening at once. He reached for her hand, rough fingers curling tenderly around hers.

For a long moment, neither of them spoke. The silence was no longer strained, just full of everything they hadn't said.

Then, as she shifted to lean into him, his arm came around her shoulders… and he paused.

Daniel cupped her face gently, his calloused thumb resting just beneath her eye.

"I never stopped loving you. Even when I didn't know how to help."

Tears welled in Katie's eyes. "I know."

He pulled her close, and this time, she came willingly, curling into the safety of his arms. No fanfare. No grand declarations. Only the quiet comfort of two souls choosing each other again, after the storm, and in spite of it.

His hand rested lightly on her middle. Noticed. Hesitated. Moved again, slower this time, as realization dawned.

His eyes searched hers.

She met his gaze with a measured breath. "I'm with child."

Emotion flashed across his face. He looked down again at her belly, where his hand now lay still, reverent.

"Why didn't you tell me?"

She turned slightly, enough to face him, but kept her hand pressed over his. "Because I didn't know how I could handle it. I didn't even know if I could say it out loud without falling apart."

He waited, letting her find the words.

"When I had Danny, it was harder than I thought. After *Mamm* died… I couldn't tell what was heartache and what was just me being broken inside. The midwife thinks most of it started with postpartum, like something just came loose in me, and everything got jumbled up."

Daniel's brow furrowed.

"I should've told you sooner. But I needed to wrap my arms around it first. I needed to believe that I could love another child… without being afraid."

"How long have you known?"

"A few weeks. Maybe a little more."

He let out a slow breath and inclined back. The mattress creaked under his weight as he shifted away from her, dragging his hand through his hair.

"And you didn't think to tell me?"

"I didn't know how," she sighed. "I was scared."

"Of me?"

"*Nee*. Of what it meant." Her voice cracked. "Of whether I'd break under the burden of one more thing."

He looked away, jaw working. "I've been breaking too, but I didn't leave. I didn't shut you out."

"I'm sorry."

"That doesn't fix it."

She nodded. "I know."

Daniel stood abruptly and picked up the pillow he'd just set down minutes before.

Katie sat up straighter. "Daniel—"

"I need some time." He didn't turn to face her. "I'm glad you told me. But that doesn't mean I know what to do with you keeping it from me for so long."

Her hands clutched the quilt in her lap. "Where are you going?"

"Back downstairs."

He reached the door, then paused, just long enough to glance back.

"You should've told me."

Then he left.

Katie sat in the quiet, blinking against the dark, one hand resting on her belly where his had been. The silence pressed in, thicker than before. His absence was one thing, but knowing she'd driven him to it again settled in her chest like a stone.

***

The kitchen was already warm when the scent of burned toast curled through the air. Daniel stood at the counter, coffee in hand, jaw tight as he flipped the stove burner off with more force than necessary.

"Sorry, I didn't mean to burn it," Katie reached for the butter dish.

Daniel didn't answer. He poured the coffee into a mug, then set it down harder than he needed to.

Mary was already at the table, her eyes darting from one parent to the other. Ella sat with a slice of bread in her hand, chewing slowly, sensing the tension.

Katie moved to the sink to rinse a pan. "I'll make another batch."

Daniel finally spoke, his voice clipped. "Don't bother."

She stilled.

"You should've told me," he added, not looking at her.

"I know."

"I'm your *mun*. Not some neighbor you can keep secrets from."

She turned, drying her hands. "I wasn't trying to shut you out—"

"But you did."

The words weren't shouted, just firm. Cold. The kind that sank deeper than anger.

He grabbed his coat from the peg and nodded once at the girls. "I'll be at the barn."

The door closed behind him with a quiet finality.

Katie stood there, stunned but not surprised. She stared at the table where his Bible sat in its usual spot.

***

The rest of the morning passed in a quiet that no longer felt safe, only restless. The baby napped in his cradle, cheeks flushed with sleep. The girls had eaten their simple meal without her prompting, dressed themselves in coats, and slipped outside.

Katie wiped down the counters again, though they were already clean. Her thoughts scattered, refusing to land. The house sat too still, empty in the wrong places, and somehow smaller than it had been the day before.

From the window above the sink, she caught a flicker of movement beneath the old maple. Ella's bright laughter rang through the air as she flung snow into the sky. Mary twirled with her, arms wide, head tipped back to catch snowflakes on her tongue, just a little girl again, not a caretaker.

Katie sat at the table, a half-filled mug of cold tea beside her, a scrap of folded paper in her hand.

She took a breath and began to write.

*Daniel,*

*You were right. I should have told you. About the baby. About how scared I was. I don't know why I thought keeping it to myself would somehow protect you. Maybe I just didn't want to say the words out loud and make it real.*

*Do you remember that spring when we were first married and the creek overflowed? We lost the whole tomato patch, and I cried like a fool over a bunch of plants. You just took my hand and said, "We'll plant again."*

*You always knew how to start over. I didn't realize until now how hard that can be.*

*I miss us.*

*I'm sorry for the silence. For the snapping. For the way I disappeared while standing right next to you.*

*I want to find our way back. If you're still willing.*

*Katie*

She folded the note and tucked it in his Bible.

# CHAPTER 11

The winter sun had barely lifted over the rooftops when Katie and the children made their way down the snowy lane toward her father's house to clean. The girls trudged through the crusted drifts in their boots, cheeks pink, their mittened hands swinging at their sides. Danny sat bundled tightly against her chest, pressed beneath her shawl in a snug wrap.

Mary skipped ahead, eyes bright. "Do you think *Grossdoddi* will have peppermint drops in his pocket?"

Ella, dragging her scarf behind her, squealed, "*Jah*!"

Katie smiled softly, despite the weight swelling inside. Her father had always tucked sweets into his pocket for the *kinner*, a quiet way of saying "I see you" without many words. As they reached the porch, Mary raced ahead and knocked eagerly. Levi answered with a kind grin and bent down, reaching into his pockets as the girls swarmed him.

"Ah, I was nearly robbed before I opened the door," he chuckled, pulling out two striped peppermints and a wrapped butterscotch.

The girls squealed their thanks and ran ahead into the familiar kitchen. Katie followed more slowly, taking in the chipping paint and the familiar creak of the porch boards beneath her boots.

Inside, the warmth embraced her like a memory.

Even after all these months, *Mamm's* scent, lavender and bread dough, lingered in the corners of the house. Her presence clung to the quilt folded over the back of the rocker, the tin of sewing notions on the shelf, the smudged prayer chalkboard by the sink with one final scribbled verse still visible: *The joy of the Lord is your strength.*

Levi set his coffee cup in the sink. "The boys need a hand in the barn. Think you can manage the crew here without me?"

Katie nodded, grateful for the alone time. "Go on. I thought I'd start in the kitchen and see how far I get."

She hung their wraps near the stove and sent the girls to the front room with coloring books. After settling Danny in a playpen her mother always kept in the corner of the room, she turned toward the kitchen, rolling up her sleeves.

The dishes in the sink had gathered like snowdrifts, still and waiting. Dust clung to the window ledge. A thin film covered the counter where *Mamm* had once rolled out pie crusts with practiced grace.

Katie worked in silence, the rhythm of warm water and dish soap soothing her frayed nerves. She swept the floor, cleared the table, and wiped down the cabinets, her movements methodical, almost reverent. Every so often, she'd pause and let her fingers trail across something, *Mamm's* old apron still hanging on a hook, the tea towel she embroidered with cornflowers years ago.

In the front room, she paused by the rocker and ran her hand over the worn wooden arms as she sank into the seat slowly, as if seeking permission. She folded her hands in her lap, breathing in the quiet.

On the nearby stand, her mother's Bible sat like an invitation. It was worn, the leather soft at the edges, the gold lettering faded. She picked it up, ran her fingers along the cracked spine, then opened it to the pages *Mamm* had returned to again and again.

Verses were underlined in gentle pencil strokes. Notes in the margins, some in careful cursive, others scribbled hurriedly, thoughts captured in the early hours or just after supper, maybe. Ruth's voice, in ink and breath. A slip of paper fell from between the pages and floated to the floor.

Katie bent to retrieve it.

It was a torn envelope, the back of it used for a quick note…

*"When your heart is too heavy to carry, let Gott hold it for you. He made it. He can carry it."* Her mother's words, scribbled in the margin of her life, were still guiding her.

From the other room, she heard Mary's giggle, then Ella's delighted squeal as they colored together. Danny stirred in his sleep and sighed softly.

Katie closed the Bible, holding it across her knees, as though it were still warm from her mother's hands.

She stood and made her way back to the kitchen. There were still floors to mop and laundry to sort. But today, she felt her mother's presence stronger than ever.

***

The aroma of lemon oil drifted faintly through the old farmhouse, mingling with the crisp starch of freshly laundered curtains. Katie wiped her hands on a dust-smeared apron and glanced toward the table where her girls sat. A bowl of apples and fresh bread held their attention for the moment, the soft rhythm of chewing and low whispers a comfort she hadn't known she needed.

Mary traced circles into the table with one finger, her expression far too thoughtful for a little girl. "*Mamm*?"

"*Jah*?" Katie inclined forward, instantly attuned to her daughter's tone.

Mary didn't look up. "If I close my eyes, I can still see *Grossmammi* sitting in her rocker. I can almost hear her humming. Sometimes I pretend she's still here." Her voice caught. "I love being in her house."

Katie's throat tightened. "It does feel different here, doesn't it?"

Mary finally looked up, her big brown eyes solemn. "At home… it's not the same. Everyone's always tired or mad. But here, it's like… like we don't need to be in a hurry. Like *Gott* lives here, too."

Katie felt her heart stutter behind her ribs. She looked over at Ella, who was quietly feeding a piece of bread to the baby and giggling when he tried to gum it. Mary's words hadn't been said with judgment, only honesty, the kind only a child could give without knowing how deep it cut.

And it hit her like a wave. Her own sadness had trickled down like cold water into the hearts of her daughters, soaking through their joy, their play, their sense of safety.

She stared at her tea, her grip tightening on the cup. The quiet hadn't been calm; it had been tension. And Mary, precious little Mary, had carried more than any child should.

"I'm glad you told me that." Katie reached over to rest a hand on her daughter's. "I needed to hear it."

Mary blinked. "Are you sad now?"

Katie shook her head slowly. "Not sad. Just... realizing I've got some fixing to do."

"Like fixing a tear in a dress?" Mary asked, ever literal.

Katie smiled. "Exactly like that. Some things just need mending, a little at a time."

The kettle whistled faintly from the stovetop, and she stood to refill her tea. As she turned back to face her children, the light from the window spilled across their faces.

The old house was still full of Ruth's memories, but now, it was also full of a yielding promise.

Katie would carry this peace home with her. She would bring back the laughter. She would be the mother they deserved again.

And by the grace of *Gott*, she'd sew the torn seams of her family back together, one thread at a time.

***

She had waited all day to find the courage. Now that the silence had settled, she wasn't sure she could find the words.

Daniel's boots thudded softly on the stairs outside, and she looked up just as he walked into the kitchen, pulling his suspenders from his shoulders. He paused when he saw her, his face unreadable.

"Tea's still warm," she offered. "I can pour you a cup."

He hesitated, then shook his head. "*Jah*."

Katie swallowed hard. "Daniel… can we talk for a minute?"

He paused, then slowly sat across from her. His eyes searched her face, but he said nothing.

She looked down at her tea, then up at him. "I know I haven't made this easy. On you. On the *kinner*. I've pushed you away more times than I can count, and I—" She drew in a slow breath.

"I can't fix everything overnight, but I need you to know I want to try."

Daniel inclined back in his chair, weariness in his eyes.

"I hear you, but you've said that before."

She winced. "I know. And I meant it then, too. I just… I didn't know how deep I'd fallen. And I didn't want to drag you into it."

"You didn't give me a choice."

The words weren't cruel… just honest. Honest enough to sting.

"I'm sorry." Her voice cracked. "I see it now. All of it. What I've let happen. What I've taken from you, your peace, your hope, your trust."

Daniel glanced away, his jaw tight. He rubbed a hand over his mouth, then nodded slowly, the minutes stretching between them.

"I'm not asking you to forgive me tonight. I'm asking you to give me a chance to prove I'm healing. That I want to be whole again, for the *kinner*, for us." She reached across the table, her hand trembling slightly. "Please, Daniel. I miss you. I miss us, and I miss you in our bed."

He looked at her hand for a long moment before pulling his from the connection.

"I miss us too. But I don't know if I can pretend like nothing happened."

She nodded, a tear sliding down her cheek. "I'm not asking for that. Just… don't shut the door all the way."

He stood and came around the table. For a moment, she thought he might take her into his arms. Instead, he leaned down, kissed the top of her head softly, then whispered, "You want me back in our bed? Show me that we're still building something worth sleeping beside."

Katie sat still long after he left the room, heart aching but not broken. She pressed her hand to her belly, breathed a prayer for strength, and finally, quietly, carried her cup in the front room with the girls.

***

Daniel eased onto the chair near the hearth, the warmth of supper still lingering in the air. The girls were sprawled on the floor, wrapped in a quilt as Katie read from one of their favorite books. Her voice had a rhythm again, not quite the same as before, but steadier. Grounded. Almost like she was trying.

He reached for his Bible, thinking he might find comfort in a psalm or proverb. When he opened it to the last marked page, something slipped free and fluttered into his lap, a small, folded piece of paper.

His brow furrowed. He picked it up slowly, fingers brushing the familiar handwriting.

Katie's.

As he read, the background noise of the room softened to a blur. Her words sank deep:

*"I miss us. I'm sorry for the silence… Do you remember that spring when the creek flooded? You told me, 'We'll plant again.' I want to try again too, if you're still willing."*

His grip tightened gently on the paper.

He leaned forward, elbows resting on his knees, staring into the fire as the note trembled slightly in his hands. The girls giggled behind him as Katie finished the story with ease.

Daniel closed his eyes for a moment, breathing in slowly.

"*Dear Lord,*" he whispered, "*help me not to rush her. But help me not to miss this either.*"

The storybook snapped shut. Katie's voice drifted gently through the room as she urged the girls toward the stairs.

Then, as she stood and gathered the quilt from the floor, she looked up.

Daniel turned slightly and caught her eye across the room.

For just a heartbeat, the noise faded. The children's voices blurred. The flickering fire cast warm shadows along the floor.

They simply looked at each other.

No words. No apology.

But everything was in that glance, the ache, the history, the fight to love in the aftermath of sorrow. A husband and wife remembering who they were beneath a great challenge.

Katie looked down first, brushing a hand across Ella's shoulder. Daniel swallowed hard, the note still in his hand.

Mary circled back and stopped beside him, her eyes hopeful.

*"Datt?"*

He looked down at her soft face, so much like her *mamm's*.

"Will you tuck us in tonight?"

He nodded. "I'll be right up."

As she scampered off, Daniel lingered another moment, eyes returning to the folded note.

Maybe healing didn't come in one big moment. Maybe it came through glances like that. Through a wife's reaching words, a child's soft voice, and a quiet choice to keep showing up. Perhaps it began there, in the silence, in the ember of a shared glance, where forgiveness started to take root.

***

The girls' giggles had faded up the stairs, followed by Daniel's soft murmur of getting them ready for bed. Now and then, Katie could still hear Ella's squeaky protests or Mary's tired laughter, followed by the creak of the bedroom floorboards as Daniel moved between their beds.

Still, her heart was heavy. Daniel hadn't come back to her. He hadn't retreated from her either, not exactly. But he hadn't joined her after tucking in the girls. She heard him settle onto the daybed in the kitchen, quietly, without fanfare, just as he had done so many nights before.

She didn't blame him. He had every reason to be cautious. Every reason to wait. For months, she'd met his patience with silence. His love with distance. His efforts with withdrawal. She had pushed him to the very edge, and still he'd remained. But now, when she was finally ready to reach for him, he was the one unsure.

Katie closed her eyes and released a breath that carried more than just the moment. The rift between them lingered in the quiet, and she knew, this break, this ache, it was hers to mend. Words wouldn't be enough. Not now.

He needed more than promises. He needed to see that she was truly returning, not just to the house, or the routine, or even to the children, but to him. To them.

She glanced toward the door. How many nights had Daniel sat alone, waiting for her to come back to him?

She would show him.

In the morning, she'd get up and make breakfast with joy in her heart. She'd meet Emma at the bakery and stay for more than an hour. Maybe help with her *kinner*. Something simple. Something solid.

It would be small, at first. It was in folding the clothes and tucking the corners of their bed. It was in showing up for supper and not letting Mary pour the milk. It was in listening. In reaching. In trying.

And maybe one night soon, not tonight, but soon, Daniel would return to their bed, not because she asked, but because he knew he could trust her heart again.

And for the first time in a long while, Katie prayed, not because she was lost, but because she was slowly finding her way home.

"*Help me, Lord,*" she whispered into the night. "*Show me how to love him well.*"

# CHAPTER 12

The subtle note of hay, leather, and the lively breath of horses had always been a kind of comfort to Daniel. He moved slowly down the center aisle, stroking the neck of a new gelding they'd just brought in from Sugarcreek. Skittish still. Too quick on the bit. But he'd come around with patience.

"Steady, now," Daniel murmured, running a brush along the gelding's flank.

The sound of boots on packed earth made him turn.

"Daniel."

He recognized Bishop Schrock's voice before he saw the man step into the dim barn light. The bishop wore a heavy coat, and his black hat was dusted with snow. His breath fogged in the cold air as he approached.

"Bishop." Daniel gave him a nod and gestured toward a bale of straw. "You're welcome to sit.

"*Nee*, I won't be long." The bishop removed his gloves slowly, his eyes taking in the horses and the neat rows of tack hanging on the wall. "It's peaceful out here. Real work has a way of calming a man."

Daniel's hands stilled on the gelding. "Some days more than others."

The bishop tilted his head slightly, studying him. "How's Katie?"

Daniel exhaled through his nose. "Better. I think." He reached for a halter and began adjusting a strap that didn't need adjusting. "It's been a long winter."

The bishop nodded slowly. "Loss shakes a family, even more than most want to admit."

Daniel appreciated the words but said nothing and nodded.

"I came to talk to you about someone, a teenage boy."

Daniel looked up.

"His name's Eli Fisher. Sixteen. He's struggling. Acting out. Skipping his apprenticeship. Getting caught with *Englisch* boys. His *mamm's* worn down, and his *datt*…" The bishop sighed. "Well, he's the sort who thinks a harsh word fixes everything."

Daniel grunted, shaking his head. "That only drives a boy deeper into trouble."

"*Ach.*" The bishop's voice grew undemanding. "That's why I thought of you."

Daniel's brow furrowed. "Me?"

"You know what it's like to walk the edges of the world. To feel like you don't belong anywhere. You've seen what anger and shame can do to a young man. And you've come through it."

Daniel leaned on the stall gate, brushing hay from his sleeve. "I'm no example, Bishop. Not right now."

"You're exactly the kind of example he needs. A man who isn't perfect, but who keeps showing up. That speaks louder than sermons." He paused. "I was thinking maybe he could come by the barn. Help you with the horses a few days a week. Hard work. Routine. A place to feel useful."

Daniel rubbed the back of his neck. "That's not a bad idea, but I'm not too sure Katie could take another person underfoot just yet."

The bishop's expression warmed. "I've already asked Levi if the boy could stay with him. He said yes before I finished the sentence. Told me it was time that house had some noise again."

Daniel chuckled softly. "That sounds like him."

"I know you've got your hands full. But maybe pouring into someone else is what you need right now."

Daniel didn't answer right away. Maybe this was what he needed. Not to escape, but to remember who he was. To be needed by someone who wasn't expecting him to fix everything, just be there.

"What's the boy like?" Daniel asked.

The bishop stood. "Angry. Doesn't look you in the eye much. But he's smart. Strong. Deep down, I think he's just scared."

Daniel gave a slight nod. "Alright. Let him come."

"*Goot.*" The bishop smiled and reached for his gloves. "I'll tell his *mamm*. And I'll be praying. For both of you."

Daniel watched him go, the old man's footsteps crunching toward the lane as snow began to fall again.

He turned back to the gelding and patted its neck. "Looks like we've got another wild one to settle."

***

The soup had cooled in its bowls. Steam no longer curled above the pale broth, and Katie stirred her spoon in slow circles, not really tasting the potatoes or carrots she'd chopped with tired hands just an hour earlier. Across the table, Daniel wiped crumbs from the corner of Ella's mouth and handed her another half-slice of buttered bread. Katie could sense Daniel had something on his mind, and she was half afraid to ask.

It should have been a tender moment. Their family gathered again. Everyone was seated at the table. But the tension still hovered like a veil not yet pulled away.

Katie cleared her throat, glancing toward him. "You're awfully quiet today."

Daniel gave a small grunt and reached for his mug. "I've been thinking."

That wasn't unusual. He was always thinking, always carrying something unsaid. But the tone in his voice made her stop and give him her full attention.

"I had a visit from Bishop Schrock this morning," he began, his eyes fixed on the steam rising from his coffee cup. "He came to talk to me about a boy."

Katie blinked. "A boy?"

"A troubled one. Sixteen. Eli Fisher. His *datt's* hard on him, too hard, I reckon. The bishop thinks he's heading toward trouble if someone doesn't step in."

She tilted her head slightly. "And what's that got to do with you?"

Daniel looked up at her then, something discreet but firm in his eyes. "He asked if I'd let the boy work with me. A few days a week. Maybe more, if it goes well."

Katie opened her mouth to respond, but Daniel held up a hand. "I know it sounds like extra weight, especially now. But this ain't just about breaking horses. This boy… he reminds the bishop of me."

That gave her pause.

Daniel leaned back in his chair, his thumbs drumming on the chair arms. "You know how it was for me before. Angry all the time. Lost. Didn't feel like I belonged anywhere. This boy's carrying that same weight." He looked at her again. "But the bishop's right. If someone hadn't taken a chance on me… if I hadn't had someone show me what it meant to work, to belong, I wouldn't be here now. Not with you. Not with our family."

Katie watched his face. His words carried a quiet intensity, something deep, shaped by experience and anchored in conviction.

"I want to help. Not to save him. I'm not anyone's savior. But maybe… maybe I can show him there's more to this life than feeling like you're not good enough."

"And you think he's committed to the *Ordnung*, or is he teetering on the fence?" Katie asked, not sharply, just carefully.

"He needs to see it lived out. Not preached. He needs to feel it." Daniel's voice softened. "And who knows? Maybe we need him as much as he needs us."

Katie stared at her hands. The idea of welcoming a stranger into their home, into their healing, felt like a risk. They were still rebuilding, piece by fragile piece.

But then she thought about Daniel, how far he'd come. How deeply he understood pain, and how he became a better man in the process.

"Where would he stay?" she asked.

"With your *datt*. Bishop already asked him." He gave a faint smile. "He said yes before the bishop could finish the question. Said the house needed someone knocking around again."

Katie gave an easy laugh at that.

The children were giggling now, something about the baby burping and Mary blaming it on Ella. The moment swelled around her, full of mess and sound and life.

She looked back at Daniel. “Alright. Let him come. Maybe a boy like that just needs a place to be wanted. And maybe we need a reminder of what second chances look like.”

Daniel reached for her hand across the table. “*Denkie*.”

Katie squeezed his fingers. “Maybe he’s not the only one who needs something to focus on besides himself.”

***

The knock came just after the noon hour, sharp and sure on the back kitchen door. Levi wiped his hands on a towel and opened the door to find Bishop Schrock standing there, one hand on the shoulder of a lanky, broad-shouldered boy with sandy hair tucked under a well-worn wool hat.

“This here’s Eli Fisher,” the bishop stepped inside. “I believe you’ve been expecting him.”

Levi offered his hand. “I have. Welcome, Eli.”

The boy looked at the floor before slowly raising his head. He had strong shoulders and eyes that darted quickly, as if tracking every sound and shadow in the room. He took Levi's hand, grip uncertain but respectful.

Daniel entered from the hallway and greeted them both with a nod. "Glad you made it."

Eli only nodded back, silent and stiff. He stood tall—taller than both men, but somehow managed to shrink into himself, like a giant afraid of his own size. His posture wasn't prideful, just guarded like a caged animal. Built to run but too used to being trapped to trust open air.

"Come in," Levi motioned toward the long pine table. "Let's sit for a minute before I show you your room."

The bishop nodded in Eli's direction before stepping back toward the door. "I'll leave you in Levi's capable hands. You've got a fresh start here, don't waste it."

Eli's jaw twitched as he nodded again, but no words came.

When the bishop left, Levi moved slowly, not in a hurry. He knew better than to fill the quiet with noise. Some boys took time to find their voice.

He sat across from Eli and folded his hands.

"This ain't a strict house, but we've got rules. Not for punishment. Just so everyone knows what's expected and what keeps us all steady." His voice was calm but firm.

Eli glanced at him, then away again.

"You'll have your own room upstairs. The bed's made, and there's a small dresser. Keep it tidy. I won't be checking it, but it's good for a man to care for his things." He paused. "No wandering off the property without asking. I won't chase you down, but I'll know if you're missing."

Daniel stepped forward, voice even. "Don't go around the horses unless me or Samuel are with you. Some of them are still high-strung. I'd rather you not get kicked your first week here."

Eli's lips curved faintly at that, though it faded quickly.

Levi continued. "We watch out for Samuel's and Daniel's little ones around here. The *kinner* are curious, and they like to follow folks around. Especially the barn. If you see them near the stalls, keep an eye out. You don't need to entertain them. Just make sure they stay safe."

Eli gave the smallest of nods.

Daniel added, "Morning chores start early. Don't wait for a bell. You're expected to work hard, but we won't ask for more than we give ourselves."

Levi shifted in his chair. "And bedtime's at nine. Earlier if you're tired. No sneaking out, no nonsense. You're here because someone believes in your worth. Don't forget that."

That made Eli flinch slightly, like a truth had landed where he wasn't expecting it.

Levi leaned back. "This ain't the kind of place where we raise our voices. I won't yell. But I will expect you to listen. You do your part, and we'll do ours. Understand?"

Eli finally spoke, voice hoarse and low. "Yes, sir."

Levi nodded once. "Good. Your room's at the top of the stairs, first door on the left. Supper's at five. You're welcome to eat with me, or not. Up to you. But this house runs on family, and you're part of it now."

Eli looked between the two men, uncertainty in his expression, but something else too, relief, maybe, or confusion at how calm things felt here.

Levi pointed toward the stairs. "Go on up and get yourself settled."

The boy hesitated, then picked up his bag and made his way up the stairs, footsteps heavy but unhurried.

Levi and Daniel sat in the stillness that followed.

"He's got pain in his bones," Levi murmured. "You can see it in how he walks."

Daniel nodded, watching the staircase. "And fear in his eyes."

"Remind you of anyone?"

Daniel smiled faintly. "*Jah.*"

Levi looked toward the window, where the low January light spilled over the fields. "He's been through more than he'll say. Just like you were."

"*Jah.* He needs something to belong to, and someone who won't give up on him."

Levi looked at his son-in-law. "You still got that fight in you?"

Daniel met his gaze. "I reckon I do."

Levi smiled. "Then let's give that boy something worth staying for."

***

Daniel walked out into the crisp night air, pulling the barn door shut behind him. The snow had started again, a light dusting that softened the hard edges of the farm. He slipped his hat back on and shoved his hands into his coat pockets, his breath rising in misty clouds.

Eli was at Levi's, silent, uncertain, and raw with something Daniel recognized too well: a boyhood built on fear and loneliness.

He walked a few steps down the lane and paused by the fence line. Beyond it, the wide open fields of Willow Springs stretched out, still, peaceful, and nothing like the city streets where he'd grown up.

The memories came faster than he wanted.

Sleeping in a hallway at the age of seven, afraid to close his eyes because the older boys in the foster home might come looking for trouble.

A cracked photograph of his mother was tucked under a floorboard, her eyes hollow from years of pain and regret. The sick smell of beer on his father's breath, and the sound of fists hitting the wall when Daniel wasn't fast enough to disappear.

He'd spent years believing he had no one. Until *Gott*, in His mercy, led him here, to this peaceful, snow-covered land, to a sister he didn't know he had, and a community as if he was born to belong there.

And Katie. A girl with a serene faith and stubborn grace who had seen past all of it, his fear, his failures, and believed there was something in him worth loving.

He leaned against the fence and tipped his head back, eyes scanning the dark clouds overhead. For a long time, he hadn't known how to forgive the lies, the resistance, the years lost to other people's choices.

And now… he saw a boy inside Levi's house who might be walking that same narrow ledge between rage and redemption.

Maybe mentoring Eli was more than just a request from the bishop. Maybe it was *Gott's* way of giving Daniel something he'd found himself, someone to pull him off the ledge.

He pushed off the fence and turned back toward the house. The porch light glowed ahead of him, with Katie and the girls inside. It wasn't perfect. It was still broken in places. But it was his and it was where he called home.

***

The early morning fog clung low to the pasture, the ground damp beneath Daniel's boots as he walked toward the barn. A faint snort greeted him from inside, the bay gelding, already awake and restless in his stall.

He reached for the latch and pushed the heavy door open with a creak. Inside, the air was warm with the scent of hay, leather, and horse sweat. Eli stood near the far wall, back straight, arms crossed tightly over his chest. He hadn't moved a muscle since Levi sent him out ten minutes earlier with instructions to wait for Daniel. He stood stiff and still, like a statue carved from stone.

Daniel cleared his throat. "You've been around horses much?"

Eli shrugged, eyes fixed on a spot in the hay-covered floor.

Daniel walked slowly toward the tack wall, giving the boy space. "You act scared around them, they'll feel it. You act like you're in charge when you're not… well, they'll remind you who's heavier."

A flash, just a small one passed across Eli's face. Not a smile. Not even a smirk. But something less guarded.

Daniel kept his voice even. "I wasn't raised Amish, even though my father was. Didn't grow up with animals, not like most boys around here. The first time I touched a horse, I was sixteen. Thought I could handle him. Got thrown so hard I saw stars for two days straight."

Eli glanced at him then, just a flick of his eyes. Fast. Nervous.

“That one there—” Daniel nodded toward the stall, “—is Cooper. Fast, strong, but skittish. Came from a family that didn’t know how to handle him. Doesn’t trust easily. Same as you, I reckon.”

Eli sighed.

Daniel leaned against a post, crossing his arms. “Levi says you’re quiet.”

Then, low: “I don’t trust people much.”

Daniel nodded slowly. “Neither did I when I was your age.”

That hung in the air between them.

Daniel didn’t push. He grabbed a pitchfork and started mucking the nearest stall. After a minute, he heard the scrape of boots and looked up to see Eli had picked up a rake.

No words. Just a noiseless gesture that said, I’m willing.

They worked in silence for several minutes. Daniel kept an eye on him, not in a suspicious way, just observant. Eli was strong and careful, but his movements were rigid like he expected to be corrected. Or worse…

“Work’s honest here. We don’t shout unless there’s a fire. And no one lays a hand on anyone. Not ever.”

Eli's shoulders eased a fraction.

Daniel nodded toward the feed bins. "Go ahead and prep the grain buckets. I'll bring Cooper out to the paddock."

Eli hesitated, looking unsure.

"You'll get the hang of it. And if you don't, I'll teach you. That's the deal. You're not here to be perfect. You're here to learn."

Eli blinked a few times, then gave the slightest nod Daniel had seen in his life. It was enough.

Daniel watched him shuffle toward the bins, stiff and uncertain but moving. The boy reminded him of a stray dog, starved, suspicious, desperate to belong but too afraid to ask for it.

As he looped Cooper's halter over the gelding's head and led him out into the paddock, Daniel whispered under his breath, "*Help me soften his blows, Lord.*"

# CHAPTER 13

The snow was pulling back from the edges of the road like a tired blanket being folded away. Slushy puddles soaked into the earth behind the bakery, and the first hints of spring clung to the air… almost hopeful.

Inside the bakery, the lingering essence of rising dough mixed with the maple-sweet promise of spring. Emma stood at the long wooden counter, kneading a batch of honey wheat bread while Katie checked the maple sugar cookies baking in the oven.

Behind the gingham curtain at the rear of the shop, the muffled sounds of children laughing and squabbling drifted through… six *kinner* tucked safely in the play corner, their boots drying on old flour sacks by the stove.

For the first time in months, Katie felt something close to peace. Maybe it was the warmth of the oven, or the way the wooden spoon fit her hand again without feeling foreign.

Maybe it was the way Emma moved beside her, sure and steady, like she always had. Or maybe it was simply that, with their hands busy and hearts quieted, they didn't need to fill the space with words.

Still, Emma was the first to speak. "I saw the daffodils by the side wall this morning."

Katie looked up, the mention of them tugging at her. "The ones *Mamm* and I planted last spring?"

Emma nodded. "Two little green shoots poking through. Brave things, ain't they?"

Katie smiled faintly, her eyes stinging just a bit. "She said they'd come back, even if it snowed late."

Emma's hands stilled in the dough, her gaze gentle. "She was right about a lot of things."

For a moment, neither spoke. Outside, a wagon creaked by on the thawing road. A bird chirped tentatively from the eaves. Then Emma turned, wiping her floury hands on her apron.

"I was wondering," her voice was low, "how are you feeling these days? Truly."

Katie didn't answer right away. She reached for the tray of cooling cookies and began placing them carefully on a linen-lined rack in the case. Her movements were slow, thoughtful.

"Tired," she admitted finally. "But... not like before."

Emma tilted her head. "Different kind of tired?"

Katie looked at her and gave a small, knowing nod. "A private tired. The kind that comes with... growing."

A gentle smile spread across Emma's face. "So then... I suppose I'm not the only one hoping for a summer baby."

Katie blinked, then gave a breathless laugh. "You too?"

Emma's smile turned shy as she leaned on the rim of the counter. "*Jah.* Only Samuel doesn't want to make a fuss just yet. But I figured you'd understand."

"I do," Katie's hand instinctively rested low against her belly. "Daniel knows, but it's still something I'm holding close."

"Some blessings grow best in quiet soil," Emma murmured.

"Like daffodils," she uttered.

Emma followed her gaze. "*Jah.* Just like that."

From the back of the bakery came a crash and a burst of laughter. Ella had knocked over a basket, and Mary was already helping her gather up the scattered blocks. Emma sighed, grinning.

"Better check on them before Otto puts a cinnamon roll in Danny's nappy again."

Emma chuckled as Katie walked away.

***

Emma leaned both hands on the counter, her breath shallower than usual. She hadn't said anything to Katie, not yet. Maybe it was just nerves or the pressure of so many long days. Still, a trace of dread had been tightening in her low abdomen for over a week now.

The baby hadn't moved. Not since that flutter two weeks ago… or was it three, and just that morning, the slightest of spotting had alarmed her.

She rested a hand under her belly, eyes distant. It had happened once before. A fall down the stairs in her first year of marriage. A small, silent grave. A wound that had never fully closed. The thought of reliving that pain again—

She closed her eyes, trying to will it away. "*Nee*, not again."

Behind her, the muffled chatter in the back room rose and fell like a tide. The laughter of the girls out front usually brought her comfort, but today it grated, like a sound too bright for a heart shadowed by fear.

Katie returned from checking on the children. "Everyone's playing nicely," Katie slipped behind the counter. "Mary has been doing a lot of stuff for Ella without a fuss. That might be a miracle."

Emma tried to return her smile, but the pain hit too fast, low, sharp, and deep. Her knees buckled slightly as she doubled over, grabbing the edge of the counter with a gasp.

Katie rushed to her side, steadying her. "Emma?"

Emma's face had gone pale. Her hand pressed protectively to her side.

"It's the baby," she sighed.

Katie's breath caught.

Another wave of pain swept across Emma's features, but she straightened slowly, swallowing hard. "It's not like last time. I didn't fall. I just… I haven't felt movement. And now this."

Katie guided her to a stool behind the counter.

Tears welled in Emma's eyes. "I thought I could ignore the fear. But it's creeping in like it did before. Like when I lost him…"

"I'll go get Samuel."

Emma looked down at her friend, her shoulders shaking with the effort to hold herself together. "You've had your own valley to walk through, and I didn't want to add to it."

"We carry each other's burdens."

Emma's eyes filled again, and she nodded slowly, grateful beyond words.

***

The early spring wind nipped at Katie's shawl as she ushered the five *kinner*, plus the *boppli* up the front steps of her home. Though the snow had long since melted, a damp chill still clung to the air. Patches of thawed ground revealed muddy grass and the promise of green not far off.

"Shoes off at the door," she reminded mildly, holding Danny on her hip as Mary guided Ella and Emma's twins inside.

The house filled quickly with the muted thumps of stocking feet and the rustle of coats. Emma's youngest, Cindy, curled into Katie's side without a word, thumb slipping into her mouth. The familiarity of the moment struck Katie like a memory she hadn't known she missed: warm bodies, soft chaos, the peaceful hum of life.

Daniel came in a few minutes later, his boots muddy from the barn. He paused at the doorway, taking in the unusual bustle.

"Well," he pulled off his hat, "I'd say you have a full house."

Katie gave him a tight smile, brushing a damp curl from her cheek. "Emma needed someone to take the *kinner*. It was all happening so fast, I didn't even think, just brought them back here."

Daniel nodded, his brow furrowed. "Samuel didn't say much, but you could see it on his face. He's scared."

"She is too." Katie's voice lowered. "I could tell before she even doubled over. Something's been weighing on her."

Daniel moved closer and took Danny from her arms. "You did the right thing."

Before Katie could respond, a knock came at the door. Levi stepped in without waiting, hat in hand, the early evening air still clinging to his coat.

"*Datt*?" Katie asked, already feeling the knot tighten in her stomach.

He gave a short nod. "Just came from the phone shanty."

The room grew still, save for the muffled laughter of the children down the hall.

"They're on their way back home. The baby's heart sounds strong, but the midwife said she'll need complete bed rest until the baby comes."

Katie exhaled, her fingers tightening around the back of a chair. "And the bakery?"

Levi looked at Daniel, then back at Katie. "She won't be able to step foot in it for the rest of the spring. Samuel's going to try to take care of the house and work when he can, but they'll need help. Real help."

"I'll handle it," Katie said without hesitation. "We'll figure it out."

Levi's eyes softened. "Didn't doubt it."

He moved back toward the door, then turned. "Sometimes *Gott* gives us a purpose by placing someone else in our care. And sometimes that's how He starts mending what's been broken."

Daniel nodded once in agreement, but it was Katie who felt the weight and the kindness of those words fill her heart.

After Levi left, Daniel set the baby down in the playpen and joined her in the kitchen.

"It'll be a full house." He watched as Mary and Ella trailed past with Emma's twin boys. "But it could be ours one day, six *kinner*, maybe more."

Katie met his eyes. "Oh my! Not sure I'm ready for that."

Outside, the wind rustled through bare tree branches, and somewhere beneath the old garden beds, daffodils waited to bloom. Inside, Katie felt a sense of hope and purpose in the crisis.

***

Katie was wiping flour from the kitchen counter when she heard the crunch of gravel under buggy wheels. She glanced out the window, heart thudding a little harder. The children were still finishing their lunch, the house buzzing with their chatter, and Daniel had just gone back out to the barn.

By the time Katie reached the front door, the buggy had come to a stop, and Betty was stepping down, a large bag in hand, her black bonnet tilted forward against the wind. Her face was flushed from the cold, and her wool shawl was dusted with early spring dust. She looked like she'd come prepared for a long stay.

"Betty?" Katie opened the door wider, surprised.

"Levi told me what happened with Emma. Poor dear. He also told me you're keeping the bakery going and caring for six *kinner*. Seems to me you could use a hand."

Katie's throat tightened. "I—I wasn't expecting—"

"I know you weren't. But the Lord gave me strong legs, sturdy hands, and a heart that doesn't rest well when those I care about are carrying too much." She looked toward the window, where the sound of laughter drifted from the kitchen. "It's no trouble. Truly."

Betty didn't wait to be invited in. She walked inside like someone who belonged, because by now, she nearly did.

Katie closed the door gently behind her, the flexible radiance of the house wrapping around them. "Are you sure? You've done so much already—"

"You're not the only one who cares about Emma. And you're not the only one Ruth left behind," Betty set her bag beside the coat rack. "I've got room in my heart for a few more little ones, and Levi's already offered to help where he's needed."

Katie blinked at that. "Levi?"

Betty gave her a sidelong glance. "He's a good man."

Katie nodded slowly, emotion building in her chest.

From the other room, a crash sounded, followed by giggles and a "*Nee*, that's *my* spoon!" Katie winced.

"Well then," Betty loosened her shawl and hung it on a hook. "I suppose I'd better go introduce myself again to this little tribe, and then I'll get started on those dishes."

Katie stood still for a moment longer, watching Betty move with practiced ease, tidying, straightening, humming softly under her breath. Just like that, the burden of the day felt a little lighter. Not because everything was fixed, but because once again, she wasn't carrying it all alone.

"*Denkie*, Betty."

Betty glanced up and offered a small smile. "That's what we do… take care of our own."

# CHAPTER 14

The damp chill of early April still clung to the air. Katie tugged her sweater tighter around her waist as she made her way across the lane to her *bruder's haus.*

The door opened before she even knocked. Samuel stood there, his expression weary but grateful. "She's resting, but she's been asking for you."

Katie stepped inside, her eyes adjusting to the dim light. The smell of herbal tea hung faintly in the air. Emma sat propped up on the settee, her growing belly cushioned by soft pillows, her cheeks flushed with worry.

"I came to gather a few things the *kinner* might need," she said softly. "Clothes, their little blankets, and maybe that blue stuffed horse Cindy can't sleep without."

Emma's face crumpled. "I hate this," she brushed at her tears with the heel of her hand.

"Stop. You've carried me for so long. It's alright to let me take the reins for a while. I'd say it's my turn."

Emma looked away, her voice trembling. "I just… I can't lose another baby. I couldn't survive it. I'm afraid every moment. Afraid to move, to breathe too deeply."

Katie reached for her hand. "You're doing exactly what you should. Resting. Letting your body do what *Gott* designed it to do."

"But the bakery—"

"Is under control," Katie said firmly. "You trained the girls well. They can manage the early shifts, and I'll take care of the rest. And Betty's back. She showed up yesterday with her bag in hand, already cooking supper before I could even think about it."

Emma's brow lifted slightly. "She moved back in?"

Katie nodded. "Said *Datt* told her about you being put on bed rest, and that she couldn't sit by while things needed doing. The *kinner* were overjoyed to see her. She's already got everything under control. You know how she is."

A faint smile pulled at Emma's lips. "Betty could organize a barn full of cats."

They both laughed softly, the sound fragile but real.

Katie settled more comfortably beside her. "I'll bring the *kinner* by after supper so they can see you. But you rest, Emma. That's your only job right now."

Emma's eyes shimmered again. "I hate being the one who needs help."

Katie smiled tenderly. "Funny, I said the same thing not long ago. And now here I am, telling you what you once told me: Lean into it. You're not alone."

Then Emma's expression shifted to one of discreet amusement. "So… Betty's been spending time with *Datt*. Do you suppose that will go somewhere?"

Katie chuckled. "They do seem to have a fondness for each other. I caught her folding his shirts the other day like she's been doing it forever. And he… well, he smiles a lot more. She's good for him. And he for her."

Katie nodded, her gaze thoughtful. "It's early still. But maybe, after the mourning year is over…"

Emma's eyes twinkled. "She'd make a fine match. A strong woman with a kind heart. Maybe the Lord knew what He was doing, even in all this heartache."

They fell silent again until Emma glanced out the window. "What about Eli? How's he settling in?"

Katie smiled. "Still as a shadow, but I've seen the way he watches Samuel and Daniel. Like he's trying to figure out what makes them tick. He's helping in the barn, doing his chores, and even sat with us during devotions last night."

Emma rested a hand on her belly. "You think maybe… the Lord sent him too? Not just for Daniel, but for Levi?"

Katie considered it. "*Jah.* Maybe Eli's not just here to be helped. Maybe he's here to help, too."

Emma closed her eyes, a small tear escaping down her cheek. "The Lord never wastes anything. Not even pain."

***

The warmth of the May sun filtered across the porch as it lit the rows of freshly washed diapers hanging on the line and the grass now bright with spring. The sweet smell of lilacs drifted on the breeze, filling the air with a sweetness that made Katie pause mid-sentence just to breathe it in. The bush by the porch rail had blossomed overnight, its lavender colored blooms heavy and full, just as they had been the spring before.

She sat in the rocker closest to the rail, her hands curled around a teacup, while Betty sat nearby mending one of Daniel's shirts. The children squealed in the yard, chasing one another through the green grass still damp from the morning dew. The air held a peace Katie hadn't felt in months.

Katie smiled, though her eyes shimmered with the pull of the memory. "Last year, *Mamm* and I sat right here, just like this. We drank tea and watched the lilacs bloom, and she thanked *Gott* for the beauty of His creation. I remember thinking she always saw the good, even when the days were hard." She paused, voice dipping softer. "I never thought I'd feel that again… anything close to joy."

Betty looked up from her stitching, her voice gentle. "Misery's like winter, ain't it? Long and cold, and you can't see the flowers under the snow. But they're there, waiting."

Katie's throat tightened. She looked down at her hands. "I kept trying to find my way back to who I was before. But I don't think I'm meant to be her anymore."

"*Nee,*" Betty agreed softly. "You're someone new now. Not weaker. Just wiser. Softer in the right places. And maybe stronger in others."

They rocked in companionable rhythm for a time, the lull broken only by Ella's laugh as she tumbled in the grass and Mary's little voice helping her back to her feet.

Betty set her mending aside. "Have you thought any more about the quilt?"

Katie exhaled slowly, her eyes drifting toward the sewing room window upstairs. "I have. I wasn't sure if I could finish it. We started it for Mary's birthday, but... it feels like it belongs to something bigger now."

"Maybe it does. The Benefit Auction is coming up. Could be a blessing to someone else, and a way to honor your *mamm*."

Katie's head tilted. She hadn't thought of that, not really. But the idea settled in her heart with surprising warmth. "I think... I'd like that," she said at last. "To finish it. To give it away. Maybe that's what healing looks like, giving something beautiful back to the world."

Betty smiled. "I'll organize a quilting bee. Get some of the women from the *g'may* to come lend a hand. We can sit around that frame and stitch love into every pattern."

Tears welled unexpectedly in Katie's eyes, but they were silky, not heavy. "*Dankie*, Betty. For everything."

"I'm just doing what your *mamm* would've done for someone else."

They rocked a little longer, the sun warming their faces, the scent of lilacs filling the space between them. In the yard, the *kinner* played with a kind of lightness that only spring could bring. And inside Katie's heart, something old began to bloom again.

Then, from down the road, the sound of sirens shattered the stillness. The distant wail of an ambulance, rare and jarring in their peaceful corner of Lawrence County, grew louder as it passed by the lane. They paused their rocking, eyes following the red blur as it rushed by, kicking up a cloud of dust behind it.

Katie turned her face toward the road, her smile fading.

Betty set her mending in her lap and bowed her head.

Katie followed suit, whispering a healing prayer under her breath. *"Grant mercy, Father, to whomever is hurting."*

The sound faded into the distance, swallowed by the trees, but the weight of it lingered.

After a moment, Betty picked up her needle again, her voice low. "Even on days full of light, sorrow walks near."

Katie nodded. "*Jah*… it does."

***

The hammer struck the nail with a fixed rhythm as Daniel braced the new plank against the stall post. Dust swirled in the shafts of afternoon sunlight cutting through the barn's loft slats. Behind him, Eli crouched low, holding the other end of the board in place while the skittish gelding snorted and shifted nervously in the next stall.

"She did a number on this one," Daniel muttered, more to fill the silence than anything else. "Got herself worked up over the wind in the trees, most likely."

Eli didn't reply, just kept his eyes on the plank, jaw tight.

Daniel glanced at him and then back at his work. "She reminds me of someone," he said after a beat. "Not just nervous… caged. Like she's been boxed in too long and doesn't know what to do with freedom."

Eli's hands stilled. He didn't look up, but his eyes gave him away.

Daniel drove another nail in, letting the moment hang.

"I used to feel like that," he added. "Like if I let go, I'd break something. Or someone."

Eli shifted his weight and sat back on his heels. "*Jah*… I know the feelin'."

Stillness settled over them again, heavy, but not unkind. The kind men needed for thinking.

"She's been like that long?" Eli finally asked, nodding toward the horse.

Daniel leaned on the hammer. "Since she was broke too young. Pushed hard before she was ready. She never learned to trust. Now she doesn't know what to do when someone handles her gently."

Eli ran a hand over the back of his neck, glancing toward the stall. "Some animals… some people… don't take to gentle right off."

"*Nee*," Daniel agreed, "they don't."

The wind rattled the loose barn door just enough to make both of them glance up.

"My *datt*… he drank," Eli said suddenly. Not loud, not even bitter… just flat. Like someone naming a thing that had always been in the room.

Daniel didn't flinch. "Mine too."

Eli looked up at Daniel. "He… he wasn't just hard on himself."

"Neither was mine."

The two men stood in that truth for a while, no need to say more. In Amish life, pain was rarely laid bare, but it didn't have to be loud to be heard.

"I used to think I'd end up like him," Eli replied. "Angry and lost, like there wasn't another path."

Daniel nodded. "There wasn't until I found the one that was always waiting for me to turn to."

Eli narrowed his eyes. "You mean the Lord?"

"I didn't grow up with faith like you did. Didn't even know who I was. But once I did… once I saw what Christ could carry for me, I didn't want to carry it alone anymore."

Eli stared at the hammer in Daniel's hand. "What made you believe that could be enough?"

Daniel didn't answer right away. He looked around the barn, the same barn he and Katie had built up with nothing but borrowed tools and stubborn hope.

"Because it was. When I had nothing. No name. No home. Not even a future worth claiming. He gave me all three."

He reached for another board and handed it to Eli. "You're not as alone as you think."

Eli didn't reply, just nodded.

***

A cloud covered the sun just as Levi pulled his buggy in front of Daniel and Katie's *haus* and stopped. Daniel walked out through the large double barn doors, wiping his hands on a rag, and headed to the porch to meet him. Katie came around the side of the house, a half-full basket of clean laundry pressed against her hip.

Levi's face told them the news before he even opened his mouth.

He climbed down slowly and removed his hat. His eyes were rimmed with fatigue. "Gerald Shetler passed earlier. Heart attack, they think. It was quick."

Katie stopped mid-step. Her arms tightened around the laundry basket as the breath caught in her throat.

"They've closed the grocery for the week," Levi added. Betty had come out onto the porch and quietly folded her arms, her mouth a thin line of concern as she listened to Levi's report.

For a long moment, no one spoke. The wind picked up and rustled the lilac bushes at the corner of the house, a whisper of spring in the cool air.

“It seems too soon for another funeral,” Betty’s voice was soft, almost reverent.

Daniel reached out and gently took the basket from Katie’s arms, setting it down on the porch steps. “I remember how silent it was after everyone left.”

Katie’s eyes filled with tears. “I’m not sure I can walk through that again so soon.” She looked toward the Shetler farm in the distance. “Now Leona’s going to feel that same emptiness.”

Levi gave a solemn nod. “Gerald was a hard man, but he was hers. That kind of loss hollows a *haus*.”

“I should go to her.”

Daniel looked surprised. “She wasn’t exactly kind to you after your mother passed. She may not want company.”

“She may not,” Katie agreed. “But that doesn’t mean she should be alone.”

Betty strode down from the porch. “*Gott* doesn’t ask us to wait until someone asks for help. He asks us to be willing. Especially when we understand their sorrow.”

Katie turned to her, blinking away the sting in her eyes. “What if I remind her too much of what she’s lost?”

"Then you remind her she's not the only one who's lost something," Betty said. "Pain shared is pain lightened."

Daniel laid a hand on Katie's shoulder. "Maybe start simple. A loaf of bread, a kind word. You don't have to do more than show up."

The wind tugged slightly at Katie's *kapp* strings. She stared out toward the trees, the stillness of early evening folding around them all.

"I'll bake something tonight. Maybe some sweet bread. Just to let her know she's not forgotten."

Betty smiled. "That sounds like Ruth's daughter speaking."

As they lingered there, quiet beneath the open sky, grief came back to sit with them, not as a thief, but as a memory, heavy and shared.

# CHAPTER 15

The morning air hung heavy with a chill that defied the warming sun. Though it was late spring, Thursday had arrived with a low-hanging mist and the kind of silence that blanketed the community on days like this. Funeral days.

Katie stood just outside the cemetery, her shawl pulled tight around her shoulders. She could see the gathering already forming, buggies parked along the lane, men clustered near the fence, women adjusting *kapps* and smoothing dark dresses.

Coming today had stirred something inside her…a simple dread. Gerald Shetler's passing had come swiftly, a heart attack that allowed little warning and no goodbyes. For three days, she had sat with Leona, bringing broth and tea, tidying the house, keeping the neighbors at bay when needed. Leona was still Leona, sharp-tongued and opinionated, but something in her had softened just a sliver, enough to allow Katie a place by her side.

Now, as the plain wooden casket was lowered into the freshly dug grave, the gathered community stood in a long, somber line. The men moved forward one by one, each lifting a shovelful of earth and dropping it onto the casket. The sound of soil hitting wood was dull, final.

Thud. Thud. Thud.

Katie flinched at the sound. Her throat tightened as memories crashed over her, the same rhythm, the same cold morning, the same disbelief that someone so full of life could be so… gone.

Leona stood ahead of her, straight-backed in her black mourning dress, so much like the one Katie still wore. Katie had never seen her so still. She hadn't wept, not publicly, but her stance spoke volumes.

When it was her turn, Leona stepped forward and took the shovel from the woman beside her. Her hands, though steady, trembled slightly as she lifted the dirt. She hesitated only a moment before letting it fall. Then she handed the shovel to Katie without turning around.

Katie moved into place behind her. She could feel the significance of the silence, the eyes of the community watching, waiting. The shovel felt heavier than she expected, and as she scooped the dirt, she whispered a prayer, not just for Gerald, but for Leona. For herself.

The earth hit the casket with a muffled thud, and Katie stepped back.

Leona's voice, low but firm, floated back to her. "I suppose this is how the Lord humbles us, *jah*? Makes us walk each other home."

"Some walks feel longer than others," Katie replied gently.

They stood together for a few moments, shoulder to shoulder, as the line behind them continued on. The cold from the ground seeped up through the soles of Katie's shoes, but she barely noticed. For the first time in a long time, she didn't feel like she was walking through her pain alone. She was helping someone else walk through theirs.

***

The hum of women's voices filled Katie's parents' farmhouse like music long forgotten. A patch of late morning sun spilled across the quilt frame, standing like a silent witness to the generations of hands it had seen over the years. Today, it was surrounded by love; by women whose lives had intersected through grief, friendship, and faith.

Katie sat in her mother's spot, her hand resting on the worn wood where Ruth's had so often been. The half-finished quilt lay stretched taut across the frame, the pattern delicate and precise. The last stitch her mother had made still sat in the cloth, the thread slightly curled where it had rested for months, untouched. Katie took a breath, threaded her needle, and finished that one stitch before starting the next.

Mary stood beside her, eyes wide, fingers carefully measuring off a length of thread just as Katie had shown her. "Is this long enough, *Mamm*?"

Katie smiled gently. "It's just right." She tied a knot for her daughter, then guided her small hands to begin their first stitch together.

Around the quilt frame, the other women worked quietly for a while, the gentle rhythm of needle through fabric filling the air. Betty sat across from Katie, her eyes full of simple satisfaction. Emma lay on the daybed nearby, propped with pillows and resting, but present and smiling.

Outside, the bakery girls watched over the children, their laughter floating in on the breeze like a hymn of ordinary joy.

Inside, the sewing room became something sacred — a circle of women gathered not just to stitch a quilt, but to honor the mothers who'd shaped them. As their needles moved through fabric, the conversation turned gently to the women who had taught them how to love, to serve, and to become mothers themselves.

Anna, Emma's older *schwester,* leaned in, smoothing the fabric in front of her. "My *mamm* once told me to never be afraid to step out and follow what I knew was right. Even if it meant stepping out alone. It's her voice I still hear when I need courage to move on or past something hard."

Emma's other *schwester*, Rebecca, looked up from her stitches, arching a brow at her sister. "Well, she gave you all the sweetness in the family, for sure and certain." The women chuckled, and Rebecca continued. "*Mamm* used to tell me that children… just like quilts, come in all different shapes and patterns. Each with their own purpose. Just because a child's different doesn't mean they're broken. Just unique." She nodded toward her *schwester* Emma. "*Ain't so*?"

Emma smiled. "*Mamm* always had a way of keeping peace between us. Without her, we might've stayed at odds."

Allie paused, her needle hovering midair. “I didn’t have a *mamm* like that, but my mother-in-law…” She smiled wryly. “Hard to love at times, stubborn as they come, but *Gott* used her to teach me patience, compassion. How to look past a person’s faults and see the purpose underneath.”

Savannah added next, “My mother-in-law showed me how to be part of something bigger than myself. A whole community, not just a family. She always said we all rise and fall together. And I didn’t understand that until I had to lean on that same community.”

Barbara laughed as she tightened the corner of the fabric near her side. “My *mamm* taught me how to speak up without ever raising my voice. And how to make my husband think something was his idea when it was really mine.”

The room burst into a heartfelt laughter. “I’m still working on that part,” Katie said under her breath, and more laughter followed.

Betty smiled, but her voice took on a reverent tone. “My *mamm’s* been gone more than forty years. But I sense her every day. When I bake. When I pray. When I scold a child or sing a lullaby, that woman shaped me.” She looked around the room, her eyes resting on Katie last. “Motherhood isn’t something that ends. It passes through us like a thread. Our job is to keep sewing with what our mothers left behind."

Katie blinked hard against tears. "We picked these colors together. I wanted to give the quilt to Mary when it was finished. But now I'm at peace knowing that we're going to donate it to the benefit auction. It feels like the last thing I need to do for *Mamm*."

Stillness settled over the group for a moment, peaceful, respectful, full.

Betty nodded. "You'll bless someone with it, and it will bless you in return."

Emma smiled from the daybed. "Maybe it's not just for one person. Maybe it's for every woman who's ever needed a little piece of comfort stitched with love."

Mary leaned her head against Katie's arm. "I'm happy we're giving my quilt away."

Katie leaned into her daughter. "*Jah*."

Stitch by stitch, surrounded by stories, laughter, memories, and a legacy of mothers who'd sewn faith and strength into their daughters, the quilt began to take shape.

And in that room, in the heart of Ruth's home, healing continued, leisurely, steady, and sure, just like the hands that guided every stitch.

***

Katie pushed open the screen door of the bakery with her hip, wiping her hands on her apron as the air filled with the scent of bubbling strawberry pie that followed her out. The spring air was thick with the promise of rain. The sky had that pale, silver sheen to it, the kind that made the breeze cooler than it ought to be for May.

She needed just a minute. One quiet breath.

She sat down on the front stoop, the wooden step cool beneath her, and leaned forward to tug off her shoes. Flour clung to the hem of her apron, and the ache in her feet reminded her it had already been a long morning.

Her eyes fell to the basket of mail beside the door. Betty had gathered it and left it for her earlier after picking up a loaf of bread for dinner. Nestled on top was an envelope.

Katie's breath caught. She knew that handwriting.

The return mark read "Pittsburgh." No name. Just that same gentle swirl of ink on the front. Her name, written with care. She turned it over, fingertips brushing the back flap.

She looked out toward the road. The clouds hung low, like they were crouching close to the earth, waiting. A faint roll of thunder echoed far in the distance. But Katie didn't move.

She opened the envelope.

*Dear Katie,*

*There's something I've learned over the years. Grieving doesn't always mean weeping. Sometimes it means waking up and choosing to keep going even when everything feels hollow.*

*After my mamm passed, I tried to be everything she had been. Strong. Collected. Always smiling. But it wore me thin. It wasn't until I started creating again, sewing, painting, even writing these letters, that I felt something bloom in me. Heartache and joy can live together. You don't have to choose.*

*God doesn't waste sorrow. Sometimes the deepest sadness is where the richest healing takes root.*

*Let yourself feel the good days without guilt. Bake your pies. Watch your children play. Stitch beauty into something that will last. That's not forgetting. That's honoring.*

*Grieving with joy is a holy kind of remembering.*

Katie folded the letter slowly, laying it across her lap like something treasured. A drop of rain landed on the step beside her, darkening the wood. Another followed. The air cooled even more, but the chill didn't seep into her like it used to. Instead, she breathed it in.

Strawberries and sugar still lingered on the breeze. Through the front window, she could hear the girls in the bakery laughing, tender and sweet as they loaded loaves into the cooling rack.

Katie closed her eyes for a moment and rested her hand over the folded letter.

"*Dankie*, Lord," she breathed.

For the letter that met her heart right where it ached. For the gentle nudge of hope… like her *mamm* brushing a hand across her shoulder.

The raindrops started to fall in earnest now, but Katie didn't rush back inside. She let them tap against her shoulders and cheeks, cool, soft, constant. She stood slowly, tucking the letter into her apron pocket before stepping back into the soothing heat of the bakery.

***

Katie stood by the table, folding a clean pile of laundry in a basket. One of Mary's dresses, a stack of diapers, and Daniel's barn shirt, all stacked with care. Her *bruder* had stopped to pick up the *kinner* for the evening, which gave her a reprieve from the chaos that extra children tended to bring.

The bathroom door creaked softly behind her. She turned, expecting perhaps Mary or Ella. But it was Daniel.

He stood in the doorway of the kitchen for a long moment, one shoulder resting against the frame. He looked tired, but not worn, more like a man who'd spent the day doing honest work and now stood at the brink of a decision long in coming.

Katie didn't speak.

He moved into the room, his eyes swept the peace-filled home, the folded laundry, the clean kitchen, and then landed on her.

"It's time."

That was all.

She held his eyes, breath caught in her throat, the ache of the last eight months washing through her grief, distance, guilt, and now… something tender and tranquil.

She held her breath as he crossed the room in a few long strides, not rushing, but with purpose. When he reached her, he didn't speak. He simply reached out and took the folded towel from her hands and set it in the basket.

His arms came around her, and hers slipped up around his waist. No words. No apologies. Just the gentle presence of his chest against her cheek and the deep sigh of two hearts settling back into rhythm.

Daniel tipped his forehead to rest against the top of her head, one hand lightly tracing the curve of her back. Katie clung to him, not out of desperation this time, but with something steadier. A choice. A promise.

His hand moved, resting lightly on the gentle roundness of her belly. She didn't speak, didn't need to. They had already said what mattered.

"I want this," she whispered at last, voice barely audible in the private room. "Us. This home. This family."

Daniel didn't answer with words. Instead, he pressed a kiss to her forehead, lingering for a breath longer than usual, and then gently took her hand and led her toward their bedroom.

They moved through the house slowly, quietly, like people remembering what home feels like.

When they reached the bedroom, Katie turned down the covers. Daniel set his pillow back on his side of the bed, smoothing the fabric before slipping beneath the quilt.

Katie followed, her hand finding his under the covers.

They lay in the stillness for a while, listening to the ticking of the wind-up clock on the dresser, the wind brushing the shutters, the breathing of a house slowly healing.

As sleep came to claim them, Daniel whispered only one more thing: "We'll be alright."

Katie, eyes already closed, muttered back, "*Jah*. By *Gott's* mercy, we will."

# CHAPTER 16

The sun was beginning to warm the muddy edges of the pasture as Samuel stood with a rope in his hand and a stubborn set to his jaw. Daniel and Levi leaned against the gatepost nearby, watching as one of the new geldings tossed his head and snorted, uneasy with the halter but showing signs of promise.

Eli stood a few feet back, holding a bucket and watching silently, as he often did, half in the work, half in his own head.

The morning was calm. Crisp. The kind of spring day that promised long hours and tired muscles. Then a sudden blare of a horn split the air, sharp and too loud for their tranquil corner of Pennsylvania.

Around the bend in the road, a rusted pickup truck came roaring past the Miller farm. The engine growled, windows rolled down, music blasting. Two boys leaned out the passenger side, hooting and hollering like they were at a county fair.

One of the horses reared back in the corral, eyes wide, muscles taut. Samuel muttered under his breath as he tried to soothe the animal, keeping a tight hold on the lead.

Daniel stepped into the corral, arms raised low and steady. “Easy, boy. It’s alright now.”

Eli had gone stiff. He turned his head slightly, following the path of the truck as it tore down the road and disappeared into the dip near the creek.

“Friends of yours?” Samuel asked sharply, still working the reins through his hands as the horse stomped and tossed his head.

Eli shook his head a little too quickly. “*Nee*, not anymore.”

Daniel caught the look in his eye. Recognition, unease, guilt, but Eli masked it quickly, setting the bucket down and moving toward the fence.

“They're probably just messing around,” Eli muttered, voice low. “Ain’t nothing to worry about.”

“Could’ve gotten someone hurt,” Samuel glanced back toward the road. “Spooked horses make poor workers.”

Eli nodded, eyes fixed on the ground. “I’ll clean the tack room,” he said and ducked away toward the barn.

Daniel watched him go, his gut tightening just slightly. He hadn't missed the way Eli's posture changed, how the carefree confidence he'd been slowly building over the past weeks had vanished in a blink. Daniel didn't press it, not yet, but he'd keep his eyes open.

Trouble didn't always knock on the door. Sometimes it just drove by with the windows down and the radio too loud.

From across the lane, the bakery door opened. Katie walked out onto the porch, wiping her hands on her apron, the two teenage bakery girls peering past her.

"What was that?" one of the girls asked.

Katie shielded her eyes from the sun. "I'm not sure, but it didn't belong here."

Back inside the barn, the faint shuffle of boots and the metallic clang of a tack hook signaled Eli's movements, but he didn't emerge.

A few moments later, Betty stepped up, carrying a tray of iced tea and a small plate of sugar cookies. Her brow was furrowed as she crossed the yard, her lips pressed into a tight line.

Levi took the tray from her, setting it on a nearby tree stump. He handed a glass to Daniel and then accepted one himself.

Betty didn't reach for a glass. Her arms folded across her chest, her gaze fixed down the road.

"That kind of noise doesn't belong here," she murmured. "Sounds like the world crashing in."

Daniel gave a small shake of his head. "Shook the horses near to pieces. We'll be calming them down the rest of the day."

Levi sipped his tea slowly. "It's hard to keep the outside world out, even here. Think they may have been looking for Eli."

She stepped in closer, lowering her voice. "I know you're trying to give him space, but if that boy's past is creeping down our road in a rusted-out truck, we can't look the other way."

"I'm not," Levi's tone was even. "Just letting him come to terms with temptation on his own."

They stood in silence for a moment, the spring wind brushing between them. From the bakery porch, the girls drifted back inside with Katie after a final glance toward the barn. Peace returned, slow and quiet.

Betty exhaled, her face softening. "I best get back inside to tend to the *kinner*."

As Betty turned to go, Levi looked toward the tack room where Eli still hadn't come out. One hand rested on the fence rail, fingers tapping slowly.

***

The sun had long slipped behind the trees, and Eli still hadn't left the barn since the ruckus earlier. He'd swept the feed room twice, rearranged the tack wall, and polished every bit of leather he could find. Anything to keep from going back into the house with questions hanging in the air.

He knew who those boys were. And he knew they'd be back.

Sure enough, just as the propane lights came on in the house, the low rumble of bass and engine echoed down the lane again.

Headlights cut through the trees, and it skidded to a halt just beyond the barn, its tires chewing up gravel. Two boys jumped out, hooting loud enough to wake the dead.

"Eli!" one of them called, slamming the truck door. "You hiding out with the bonnet heads again?"

The other boy laughed. "C'mon, man. We got beer, some cash, and we're heading down by the quarry. You're seriously mucking horse dung again? I thought we showed you there's a better way to spend your days!"

Laughter bounced across the barnyard like rocks thrown at glass.

Eli stood just inside the tack room, jaw clenched, hands fisted in the hem of his shirt. He didn't move.

But Levi did.

He marched off the porch, calm as ever, the glow of the barn lantern catching the silver in his beard. He walked with purpose, not anger. Not fear.

He stopped beside the truck and nodded toward the boys.

"You've made your noise. Now give the animals, and my family, a little peace."

The taller one squinted. "Who are you?"

Levi's voice remained firm. "The man responsible for this place. And that barn. And that boy."

"He's not a boy," the other muttered, crossing his arms. "He can make his own choices like a man."

Levi didn't flinch. He looked toward Eli, who stood in the shadow, silent.

"You're right, he can."

He turned toward Eli.

"No one's holding you here, *sohn*. If that's the path you want, go. But remember… every road you walk today becomes the path you'll live on tomorrow."

The air stilled. The crickets fell quiet. Eli stepped into the light. He didn't say a word, just walked past Levi and climbed into the passenger side of the truck.

The tires crunched and the taillights disappeared into the dark.

***

The truck came to a slow stop just past a blinking yellow light where the gravel met the paved road leading toward town.

Eli opened the door. "Seriously?" one of the boys scoffed. "We're just getting started."

Eli hopped down, boots landing in the dirt. "Appreciate the ride," he muttered.

They laughed again, confused and mocking, but Eli didn't turn around. He walked east, toward the farm, toward peace and the acceptance he found with Levi. The truck peeled away behind him.

An hour later, Levi's kitchen was still. Only the ticking of the old wall clock broke the hush. A faint scent of woodsmoke and fried onions lingered in the air, and the light over the kitchen table hissed over the room.

Eli walked through the side door and paused.

Levi was sitting at the table, hunched slightly, as if lost in thought. A half-eaten plate of supper rested before him, and beside it, untouched, a second plate sat waiting. Hamburger and cheese on fresh bread, a scoop of slaw, and a mug of lukewarm coffee.

Eli glanced at it, then at Levi.

"You knew I'd come back?" he asked shyly, still lingering by the door.

Levi didn't look surprised. He chewed once more, then set his fork down and wiped his mouth on a paper napkin.

"*Nee*, but I hoped."

He gestured to the plate across from him. "Sit. It's better when it's warm, but it'll do."

Eli slid into the chair without a word.

Levi took another slow bite of his own before he spoke again. "The truth is, I prayed you'd find your way back."

Eli looked down at the table, his voice low. "I didn't know if I was coming back until I was already walking."

Levi nodded slowly. "That's how it works sometimes."

A quietness settled between them, but it wasn't heavy. Just honest.

After a moment, Levi leaned back in his chair and studied the young man across from him. "There's something in you. You don't see it yet. Most don't when they're still carrying the impact of everything behind them."

Eli shifted, unsure what to say.

Levi's eyes softened. "I see a wandering spirit that wants to find home."

Eli swallowed hard.

Levi didn't push, didn't preach. He just offered the truth like a warm loaf pulled from the oven, there to be taken or not.

"You don't have to be like your past. You get to decide who you'll become. And not just once, every day."

Eli nodded. "It's hard."

"Ain't nothing worth doing that's easy."

They ate in silence for a while after that. No more words needed. Just two men, one seasoned by life, the other still shaping his path, sharing a meal beneath the light of a lantern, in a house that had lost much… but still had room to grow.

***

The next morning, Levi stepped out onto the porch, a steaming mug of coffee in his hand. The porch swing creaked slightly as he sat, setting the mug on the rail beside him. For a long moment, he simply listened to the distant lowing of cows, the rustle of birds waking in the hedgerow, the comforting sounds of a new day around him.

And then he spoke, not loudly, not urgently, just the soft murmur of a man used to being heard.

"Ruth." His voice cracked a little. "I suppose it's strange, talkin' to the air like this. But I miss talking to you. And the quiet. It's been loud lately. Too loud."

He picked up his mug and stared out over the field, his fingers wrapped around the warmth.

"Nine months? Hard to believe it's been that long."

He paused.

A moment of comfortable pause settled between them before Levi spoke again, his voice thoughtful. "It's a strange thing, ain't it? Just when you think you've lost too much, *Gott* sends new life."

Samuel nodded.

"Two new *bopplis* in this family now," Levi continued. "And one is already here. Feels like He's given us double the blessing after all this sorrow."

His eyes drifted toward the barn where Eli had gone out to start mucking stalls. "Maybe even three blessings, if you count the ones that come in different forms."

Samuel followed his gaze. "You think Eli will stay?"

"I hope so."

Samuel stood and dusted his hands on his trousers. "I'm off to tell Daniel and Katie. Thought you ought to be the first to know."

Levi nodded slowly, watching his *sohn* descend the steps with long strides. As Samuel walked back toward the lane, Levi looked to the sky once more, clear, blue, full of promise.

He murmured, almost to himself, "*Dankie*, Lord, for new beginnings."

The porch swing creaked gently as he sat back, one hand resting on the armrest. His heart, fuller than it had been in months, beat steadily in the warmth of a May morning that felt like hope.

# CHAPTER 17

A basket of thread spools sat at Betty's feet, her weathered hands working methodically, pulling the last thread tight as she stitched the binding onto the blue and yellow dahlia quilt.

Katie sat nearby at the writing desk, hunched over a sheet of crisp stationery. The tip of her pen tapped against her chin, her eyes thoughtful as she stared out the window. The men were starting to haul old machinery, secondhand furniture, and new items crafted by the skilled hands to the field on the outskirts of town. The Benefit Auction was just a week away, and every home seemed to be humming with preparations.

From time to time, Betty paused her stitching and gave Katie a look that was both amused and curious. "How many drafts have you written now?"

Katie smiled faintly without looking up. "Three. None of them says what I want to portray."

Betty tugged smoothly on the binding, smoothing the quilt flat across her knees. “Write from your heart. That’s what your *mamm* would’ve told you.”

“I know.” Katie set the pen down and rubbed her hands together, warming her fingers. “It’s just... this quilt feels like the last thing I’m doing for her. Like one final stitch to close the wound.”

Betty nodded slowly. “You’ve come a long way. Like snow melting into spring.”

The community was already building tents and setting up auction tables. The quilt deliveries would begin in just a few days, each one cataloged and displayed with care for the highest bidding. Katie thought of the families who would come out with pockets not deep, but hearts generous, knowing that every dollar would go toward the community medical fund.

That fund had helped her family when *Mamm* took sick last spring. Back then, Katie could only hold on, praying hard, hoping harder, with no way to fix what was breaking. But today, her hands weren’t empty. Today, she had something to give.

“I want to write something to go with the quilt. A memorial. Something that tells people this isn’t just cotton and thread.”

Betty leaned forward in the rocker, her voice low and gentle. "Then tell them it carries the story of a daughter learning to become a *mamm* again. Of a mother's faith stitched into every corner."

Katie blinked quickly, her eyes welling with sudden tears.

She picked up her pen and began again.

*This quilt was started last spring by Ruth Yoder and her daughter, Katie, with the intention of giving it to Ruth's granddaughter, Mary. It was left unfinished when Ruth passed into the arms of the Lord later that year. In the months that followed, this quilt sat untouched, a painful reminder of what was lost*

*But over time, stitches turned into prayer. Fabric turned into healing. With the help of friends and neighbors, it was lovingly completed in Ruth's honor to benefit the very fund that once helped care for her in her final months.*

*It is more than a quilt. It is a memorial of faith, of motherhood, and of community. May it bless the home it finds its way to, just as Ruth's life blessed ours.*

*Katie Miller*

When she finished reading it aloud, Betty's eyes shimmered. "That's the one."

A breeze rustled through the curtains, carrying a hint of turned soil and horses from the fields. Somewhere in the backyard, Mary and Ella were giggling, chasing bubbles in the late May air.

Katie looked down at the finished quilt, now folded neatly in Betty's lap. The blue petals of the dahlia pattern bloomed outward like sunbursts, stitched with the love of three generations.

***

Eli stood at the animal's flank, a curry comb in hand and a focused look on his face as he moved in long, practiced strokes along the horse's side. His movements were calm, fixed, not the same boy who had arrived tight-lipped and wary just a month earlier.

Daniel leaned over the fence, arms crossed, watching with a steady eye. "He's ready," he said to Samuel. "Both of them, I think."

Samuel glanced at Eli and gave a short nod. "Like a green horse who needs the right hand to ease the worry out of him. Not to force him, but to guide him."

Just then, the sound of buggy wheels made them all turn. Bishop Schrock pulled into the drive in his open buggy, the reins slack in his hands as his mare slowed naturally at the sight of the men and the horse.

"Afternoon," the bishop called as he stepped down.

"Afternoon," the men echoed in return.

Eli stiffened slightly but stayed where he was, giving the gelding a light pat before shifting to check the lead rope.

The bishop came around the fence rail, eyes sharp as he took in the horse and the boy standing beside it. "Is that the same skittish gelding I saw two months ago trying to climb the stall walls?"

Samuel chuckled. "*Jah*, and the same boy who wouldn't look you in the eye."

Bishop Schrock's eyes lingered on Eli a moment longer, and something like a smile twitched at the corner of his mouth. "It seems you've both been working hard."

Eli lowered his eyes respectfully and gave a small nod, saying nothing.

"Don't worry," Daniel said with a light grin, "he's more talkative when he thinks no one important is listening."

Levi joined them from the barn, wiping his hands on a faded cloth. He nodded to the bishop. “I take it you came to see how much trouble the boy’s been?”

The bishop folded his arms. “That’s right. Was expecting to find a half-torn fence, a bucked horse, and your patience frayed to a thread.”

Levi’s eyes softened as he looked at Eli. “What we found instead was a blessing in disguise.”

The bishop gave a long, considering nod. “I thought maybe he just needed a place to land. Didn’t expect him to root in.”

Eli turned back to brushing the gelding, giving them their space but clearly listening.

After a pause, the bishop added, “His *datt’s* in the counseling facility now. Word is he’s hoping to make things right when he gets out.”

Levi didn’t react immediately. His face remained thoughtful. “We’ll see. I hope by then Eli will be strong enough to stand on his own. And if his father does come around with a humble heart, maybe the boy will be ready to hear him.”

Daniel glanced at the bishop. “He’s not the same boy who showed up here.”

"*Nee*," the bishop agreed. "But I reckon sometimes it just takes the right place, and the right people, to remind a young man who he might become."

Samuel led the gelding toward the corral as Eli walked alongside, the late afternoon light catching on the worn leather of his boots and the perfect alignment of his shoulders.

The bishop turned to go but paused long enough to add, "That's a fine-looking horse. He'll fetch a good price at the auction."

Levi watched Eli walk, a slight smile curling beneath his beard. "That gelding isn't the only one ready for a new chapter."

***

Katie stepped down from the buggy, smoothing the skirt of her black dress as she helped Mary and Ella to the ground. The girls were practically bouncing with excitement. Daniel gave a half-smile as he reached for the reins.

"I'll get him unhitched and meet you at the sale barn in about thirty minutes." He nodded toward the back of the auction grounds where a row of trees shaded a long rope already strung for tethering horses.

Katie touched his arm briefly. “We’ll be waiting.”

He tipped his hat and the buggy creaked softly as it rolled away toward the designated area. Katie watched him disappear behind the tents before turning to face the spread before them.

The air buzzed with life.

To her right, the plant and flower tent overflowed with color, potted geraniums, delicate hanging baskets, and hearty flats of vegetables donated by local Amish greenhouses. Women in crisp white *kapps* wandered the aisles, careful not to knock over blooms, while children pointed out bright daisies or begged to carry home a tomato plant of their own.

A row of washing machines, cook stoves, and secondhand appliances lined the sun-warmed field to her left, gleaming beneath the June sky. Further on, rows of wooden furniture stood like sentinels: rockers, cribs, pie safes, all crafted with care and ready for a new home.

Mary tugged her sleeve. “*Mamm*, can we have ice cream later?”

“We’ll see, maybe after the quilts.”

With Betty watching over little Danny for the day, Katie felt lighter than she had in weeks. Free to soak in the event, she let herself walk slowly, hand in hand with her girls. The cadence of an auctioneer's chant carried from the far field where a crowd of men in straw hats clustered around the plows and planters, heads bent in concentration. Boys trailed behind their fathers, pointing at implements with wide eyes, mimicking the way their *datts* appraised the equipment.

To her other side, *Englisch* and Amish alike mingled easily, neighbors chatting over steaming cups of coffee, young women comparing hand pies wrapped in waxed paper, and elders catching up on the latest news from neighboring districts.

She turned in a slow circle, letting herself truly see what lay around her. The first Saturday in June. The auction was held on the same day every year, rain or shine, in the wide-open fields at the outskirts of their Northwestern Pennsylvania community. This year, the sun shone brightly. Bright enough to lift even the heaviest memories.

The big quilt barn loomed ahead, its doors wide open to let in the breeze. Inside, rows of metal chairs were already filling in front of the already full bleachers. Quilts in every shade and pattern hung like banners: log cabins, lone stars, and double wedding rings. And among them, near the center aisle, was the one Katie and the women had poured their hearts into: the giant blue and yellow dahlia quilt. Her *mamm's* last gift, in a way.

A hush of gratitude passed through her as she looked at it.

Mary squeezed her hand. “That’s ours, isn’t it?”

Katie bent low. “It is. And we’re going to see someone take it home today.”

The crowd was beginning to thicken as more families arrived, buggies pulled in from every direction, and horses were tied in orderly rows beneath the trees. Daniel would find them soon.

Katie stood at the entrance of the building for a long moment, breathing it all in, the colors, the smells, the voices rising in familiar Pennsylvania *Detisch* around her. A sense of peace and belonging covered her.

Katie eyes swept over the sea of blue and straw hats, the rows of quilts fluttering gently in the breeze, and the sturdy rhythm of the auctioneer’s chant echoing from the back field. The tantalizing whiff of roasting chicken mingled with the sweetness of funnel cakes and ice cream danced on the breeze.

The warmth in her heart surprised her. She caught sight of Daniel moving through the crowd. He didn’t rush. He didn’t wave. But their eyes met, and in that small, shared glance, everything else slipped away. What stood between them now was hard-won, history etched deep and sacred. No one else would ever carry the weight of what they'd endured… or understand the quiet strength it took to hold on when letting go would've been easier.

He came to stand beside her, close enough that his sleeve brushed hers, the brim of his hat forming a shadow over both of them. He didn't say a word, but he didn't need to.

She lowered her eyes, heart steady. Love had deepened, not around the hard parts, but through them. Maybe that was how marriage was shaped, not in the easy days, but in the weathering. In the quiet spaces. In the storms. In the steady, unseen choosing that happened day after day.

Daniel glanced sideways, the corner of his mouth lifting ever so slightly.

Katie returned the look with a smile of her own, then turned back to the barn, her heart full. They moved forward together, wordlessly slipping into the crowd.

***

The auction barn was already crowded by the time the woman from Pittsburgh arrived. Her sensible flats tapped nervously along the gravel, the sun already high and warm above the sprawling rows of tents and wagons. The air smelled of straw, roasted chicken, and fresh doughnuts, unfamiliar but comforting. She clutched her leather purse tightly under her arm, shielding her eyes with one hand as she scanned the crowd of bonnets and broad-brimmed hats.

She'd never been to an Amish benefit auction before. She'd never even been to a rural community like this. But today wasn't about comfort or familiarity; it was about honoring a woman who had changed her life without ever knowing it.

Her fingers brushed the folded piece of paper in her pocket, the last letter she'd written to Katie Miller but hadn't mailed. Something in her heart had told her to come instead.

She made her way to the quilt barn, weaving through crowds with apologetic smiles. Finding a seat was tricky, but a young woman in a tan dress scooted over and made room. The woman looked up and greeted her with a polite "Hello."

"Excuse me, I was wondering... do you know which quilt Katie Miller donated to the auction?"

The lady's eyes lit up. "The blue and yellow dahlia. It's on the back wall there." She pointed. "Beautiful, isn't it? Her *mamm* started it, and Katie finished it with the help of some of the women from our community."

The Pittsburgh woman followed the direction of her hand. There it was. Stunning. Bold blues, soft butter yellows, hand-stitched petals blooming across the fabric. Her throat tightened.

The crowd sat shoulder to shoulder in rows of bleachers, their muffled conversations blending with the singsong chant of the auctioneer calling bids on the last few pieces of furniture before the quilt auction began.

"You here for the quilts?" she asked, her tone friendly.

The woman from Pittsburgh nodded. "I am. Do you… do you happen to know if Katie is here today? I was hoping to speak to her."

The young woman turned, craning her neck slightly. "Down there. That's Katie Miller now, sitting with her husband, Daniel. Third row from the bottom, see?"

She followed where she pointed. She sat straight-backed, two little girls flanking her sides, her husband close beside them. She favored her mother. The woman looked down at her auction card, her fingers trembling slightly.

She remembered the last time she'd seen Ruth Yoder sitting next to her in a worn chair in the oncology clinic. Even then, in the thick of her illness, Ruth had radiated something...

something holy. Something she had never seen before and hadn't stopped longing for since.

She instantly loved Ruth. Her presence had filled the waiting room like light through a stained-glass window.

When Ruth passed, the clinic felt dimmer.

And now, her daughter was here, holding onto that same light, whether she realized it or not.

The auctioneer walked up to the front of the platform as a pair of young men unfolded the dahlia quilt and held it up for the crowd to admire.

"Next up, hand-stitched dahlia pattern quilt, pieced by Ruth Yoder and finished by her daughter Katie. A one-of-a-kind piece, folks. We'll start the bidding at fifty dollars..."

The Pittsburgh woman lifted her auction card without hesitation. She didn't care what it cost.

She just knew that quilt needed to be somewhere it would keep whispering Ruth's story, her gentleness, her strength, her unshakable peace.

And maybe, if she was lucky, she'd get a chance to thank the daughter who carried that legacy forward.

***

Katie hadn't expected to cry. She'd told herself all morning that it was just a quilt. Just fabric and thread. Just one small gift for a good cause. But as the bidding climbed past two thousand dollars and the auctioneer shouted, "Sold!" To the woman in the bleachers. Katie's throat closed like a vise. She then quietly slipped her way out the side of the building before the next quilt was even lifted.

Outside, the sun had reached its warmest stretch of the afternoon, but Katie felt cold.

Behind the auction barn, she found a bale of hay and sat down hard, pressing her palms against her knees to steady the wave of emotion that broke free the moment no one could see. She thought she'd prepared herself for this, for letting go. But now that it was done, something inside her ached so fiercely, it took her breath away.

The dahlia quilt was the last thing her mother had touched. She had picked every color with care, stitched the petals with her practiced hands, humming hymns as she worked. Katie had finished it in her absence, but her mother's fingerprints were still everywhere in that fabric.

And now… it belonged to someone else.

She bowed her head, squeezing her eyes shut, hoping the warm breeze might carry away the sting. The tears she swallowed were thick with a pain that wasn't fresh but still deep. Maybe it always would be.

The bustle of the auction had faded behind the barn. She had no idea where Daniel and the girls had gone, but she trusted he knew she needed this moment. He always seemed to know now.

She rubbed her fingers together, imagining the feel of her mother's stitching one last time.

Footsteps crunched lightly over gravel, and Katie quickly wiped her eyes before looking up.

It was Sarah Byler, Emma's older *bruder's fraa*. She held an envelope in her hand.

"Sorry to interrupt," offering it forward. "The woman sitting next to me in the auction barn asked if I'd give this to you."

Katie blinked and reached for it. "*Dankie*."

But before she could ask how Sarah was doing, how things were at home, or if she needed anything, Sarah had already slipped back around the barn with a slight wave. Katie made a mental note to check on her next week.

She looked down at the envelope. Her name was written on the front in a careful, familiar hand. Inside, a folded piece of stationery held words that would change everything.

*Dear Katie,*

*Your mother helped me more than you will ever know. She was the most peaceful woman I have ever met, and I wanted to do something in her honor.*

*I purchased your quilt today and will donate it to the cancer center in your mother's name. It belongs in a place where her presence still lingers. Somewhere others can feel what I felt... her comfort, quiet strength, and the affection of God's love. Thank you for finishing it. Thank you for sharing it.*

*May you grieve with joy, as your mother taught me to.*

*Many blessings,*

*Lillian... a woman who will always be indebted to your mother's kindness in my time of need.*

Katie read the letter twice, then folded it with care. The sadness had lifted. In its place was a quiet warmth, steady and full, like her mother's arms around her on a winter morning.

# EPILOGUE

The air held that golden hush only September could bring, warm enough to leave the shawl behind, but crisp enough to smell the change in the wind.

Katie stood beneath the maple tree, its leaves just beginning to flame with color. Joshua Levi squirmed lightly in her arms, his eyes drifting toward sleep. Mary, Ella, and Danny sat in the grass nearby, arranging stones and leaves around the edge of her mother's simple white grave marker.

Mary had brought a drawing, crayons, and folded paper. A crooked sun. A smiling family. And in the corner, a stick figure with a *kapp* and apron, labeled in careful letters: *Grossmammi Ruth.*

Katie swallowed past the lump in her throat.

She knelt, brushing leaves from around the simple marker.

"I brought him to meet you," she whispered, glancing down at the baby in her arms. "Joshua Levi. He's quiet like *Datt*, and strong like Daniel. You'd have loved him."

The wind picked up, fluttering her prayer strings.

"So much has happened, *Mamm*. Emma and Samuel have a new little one. Betty has become part of our family and spends much time walking our lane with *Datt*."

She smiled, soft and real. "And the quilt, your quilt, hangs on a wall for so many to enjoy."

Katie paused. "I used to wonder why *Gott* took you from us. Why He let me fall apart. But I see it now. Every unraveling has its own purpose. I'm learning to love again, not just Daniel, but life itself. And I'm learning to forgive myself, too."

Behind her, she heard familiar footsteps crunching across the path. Daniel. He didn't speak, just came to stand beside her, his hand settling softly on her back.

She leaned into him, heart full. Together, they stood in silence, the breeze whispering through the maple branches above.

Mary tiptoed closer. "*Mamm*?"

"*Jah*?"

"Do you think *Grossmammi* can see us from heaven?"

Katie looked down at her daughter, so full of questions and hope. "I do, and I think she's happy to see us smile again."

Ella tugged at Daniel's trousers. "Can we stop by the ice cream stand on the way home?"

Daniel chuckled, low and sincere. "Reckon we've earned it."

Katie turned one last time to the grave and touched the plain white stone, her fingers brushing the carved name like a benediction.

"Thank you, *Mamm*… for everything."

Then she turned and walked back down the lane with her family, toward home, toward hope, toward the next chapter.

***

*Caregiving changes everything—even marriage.*

A new season is coming for Sarah and Matthew Byler, one filled with change, responsibility, and the quiet work of love. *Sarah's Amish Season of Change* is a tender story of caregiving, faith, and a marriage that learns how to grow stronger through life's hardest days.

# WHAT DID YOU THINK?

First of all, thank you for purchasing *Katie's Amish Journey of Hope*. I hope you will enjoy all the books in this series. If you enjoyed this book and found it beneficial, I'd appreciate hearing from you and hope you will take a moment to post a review on Amazon.

If you love visiting Willow Springs, I invite you to sign up for my email list and enjoy Love Blooms at the Apple Blossom Inn:

If you would like to explore a reading order and a complete list of all the books in my collection, please visit:

# GLOSSARY

Pennsylvania Dutch "Deutsch" Words

**Ausbund.** Amish songbook.

**bruder**. Brother.

**denki.** Thank You.

**doddi.** Grandfather.

**doddi house.** A small house next to the main house.

**g'may**. Community

**goot meiya.** Good morning.

**jah.** Yes.

**kapp.** Covering or prayer cap.

**kinner.** Children.

**mamm.** Mother or mom.

**mommi.** Grandmother.

**nee.** No.

**Ordnung.** Order or set of rules the Amish follow.

**rumshpringa**. Running around period.

**schwester**. Sister.

**singeon.** Singing/youth gathering.

# ABOUT THE AUTHOR

Tracy Fredrychowski's life closely mirrors the gentle, simple stories she crafts in her writing. With a passion for the simple side of life, Tracy regularly shares tips on her website and blog at https://tracyfredrychowski.com.

In northwestern Pennsylvania, Tracy grew up steeped in the virtues of country living. A pivotal moment in her life was the tragic murder of a young Amish woman in her community. This event profoundly influenced her, compelling her to dedicate her writing to the peaceful lives of the Amish people. Tracy aims to inspire her readers through her stories to embrace a life centered around faith, family, and community.

For those intrigued by the Amish way of life, Tracy extends an invitation to connect with her on Facebook. On her page she shares captivating Amish photography by her friend Jim Fisher and recipes, short stories, and glimpses into her cherished Amish community nestled deep in the heart of northwestern Pennsylvania's Amish County.

https://facebook.com/tracyfredrychowskiauthor/

www.ingramcontent.com/pod-product-compliance
Lightning Source LLC
Chambersburg PA
CBHW050143120726
47903CB00002B/470
*9798991998840*